The Bride Wore Crimson

Also by Adrianne Lee

A Wedding to Die For

The Big Sky Pie series
Delectable
Delicious
Delightful
Decadent

The Bride Wore Crimson

ADRIANNE LEE

New York Boston

Forever Yours
Hachette Book Group
1290 Avenue of the Americas
New York, NY 10104
hachettebookgroup.com
twitter.com/foreverromance

First ebook and print on demand edition: November 2015

Forever Yours is an imprint of Grand Central Publishing.
The Forever Yours name and logo are trademarks of Hachette Book Group, Inc.

The publisher is not responsible for websites (or their content) that are not owned by the publisher.

The Hachette Speakers Bureau provides a wide range of authors for speaking events. To find out more, go to www.hachettespeakersbureau.com or call (866) 376-6591.

ISBN 978-1-4555-7418-6 (ebook edition)
ISBN 978-1-4555-8918-0 (print on demand edition)

To Drew, Trent, and Andrew Zeppa.
We faced the devil and beat him.

The Bride Wore Crimson

Chapter 1

Things were about to get insane. I heard it on the gentle July breeze, smelled it in the salty air, tasted it in my morning coffee. Think convention on steroids. In Vegas, merchants set up displays in two or three humongous buildings. Blocks long. In Weddingville, Washington, the whole town gets involved, every single business. Residents sell their yards for parking lots. Shoppers swarm the walkways and the stores, grabbing bargains, garnering ideas. Dresses fly from Blessing's Bridal faster than the showroom can be restocked. Yep, things were about to get craycray. I just didn't realize how crazy.

I hadn't been to a bridal fair in seven years, but I still knew the preparation was as important as the resulting income. Good thing I excelled at organization. *Like you did, Daryl Anne Blessing, being your best friend's maid of honor?* I cursed the little voice inside my head but winced at the accuracy of the allegation. Usually I'm levelheaded, sensible, logical. *Perfect traits in a maid of honor whose primary duty is to keep the bride emotionally calm.* My stomach pinched. I'd done a stellar job of that. Eight weeks later, my bestie Meg Reilly was still single, we'd both given up our dream jobs in Hollywood, moved back to our hometown, and into our respective parents' houses.

Practical, yes—as well as a little embarrassing.

But it wasn't my fault Meg's ex-fiancé slept with her mother... shortly after getting engaged to Meg. Not that he'd known she was Meg's mom, but still... *Loser*. And it wasn't my fault that Meg's mom was a self-centered bitch-on-wheels, or that she ended up murdered, or that Meg was shot as we tried to escape the killer.

I mean, really, how could any maid of honor keep the bride calm given all that?

Thankfully, the bullet only grazed Meg's scalp. The real damage? Grief, confusion, and trauma. Her usually bright spirit had gone into hiding. Like the sun peeking from behind a huge, dark cloud, there were a few moments of light shining through, but mostly it was gloom. She seemed to be drifting through each day. I had to snap her out of it. I wanted my best friend back, not this new, angrier version of her.

So sue me. I decided to try shock therapy. But then my conscience kicked in, and now I feared this might be rubbing salt into some pretty fresh wounds. "If you'd rather not do this, Meg, I will totally understand."

"Daryl Anne," Meg said, green eyes flashing as she gave a toss of her head, her mass of red curls bouncing, the tiny scar near the hairline showing, "everywhere I go in this seaside village, everywhere I look, I see something that reminds me. It's unavoidable."

I sighed, jabbing a hand through my super-short black hair. My gaze shifted to our surroundings, as if I could find the right words written on the old brick walls. But probably the only tales this three-story building might tell were of its former life as two warehouses and the logging company that had flourished here.

The building came to my family fully renovated, its history disrupted, the top floor turned into a single-family residence and the lower two levels repurposed for our business, Blessing's Bridal. Meg and I were on the main floor in the storeroom that separated the salon from the office and alterations. We were in the process of categorizing gowns according to price and style and placing them onto racks that would soon be pawed through by excited, determined shoppers.

I faced her again. "I know, it's impossible to avoid the reminders, but—"

"No," Meg said, stopping me mid-protest. She waved a dismissive hand. "I'm so glad to be out of the café. It's not cool when someone orders coffee and I burst into tears for no apparent reason. I think I'm doing fine, then *wham*, the waterworks start. Then comes the pity. Or the customer walks out. Compared to that, this is a piece of wedding cake."

What she was enduring sent an ache through my heart that even her pun didn't ease. I was glad she could joke, but I wanted to hug her, to take away every last ounce of distress and heartbreak and grief. I resisted the urge and squeezed her hand instead. "Are you sure?"

She gave me a smile full of gratitude and then smacked a couple of dresses. "Hey, all this lace and chiffon—"

"Tulle."

"Tulle..." Meg pursed her lips, reproof in her gaze.

I winced. *Note to self: Zip your lip.* I made that gesture and earned a goofy grin from Meg. "Sorry."

"Daryl Anne Blessing, I couldn't ask for a better friend than you." She caught both of my hands, made me look right at her. "I have to do this. I want to do it. Think of it as getting back on the horse that threw me."

I blinked, Meg's sunny light finally parting the dark clouds. Maybe this would be okay after all. "Now I'm the one who's going to cry."

"Don't you dare," she admonished.

A bell jangled, announcing someone had come through the front door. The locked front door. Meg's eyes rounded. My nerves tweaked. Mom and Gram were still upstairs in our third-floor apartment. The shop wasn't open yet. Our gazes met, alarm echoing alarm. Shivers scurried across my skin. Okay, so I was still a bit traumatized, too.

I pulled my phone from my pocket. It wasn't much of a weapon, but after almost being killed eight weeks ago, I had 9-1-1 on speed dial. We crept to the salon, me in the lead. The light in the reception area was filtered through the butcher paper taped to the three huge display windows. The main room always reminded me of a charming New York brownstone, the walls plasterboarded with patches of aged brick showing through. Original hardwood planking and high ceilings made the space seem larger than it was.

Two red velvet love seats served as the waiting area, while a rack of brochures from the various businesses in town stood near an Edwardian reception desk. The usual bouquet of fresh roses was missing from the center table, the air bereft of that lush aroma. And several naked mannequins awaited Meg's and my attention. As all of this crossed my mind, I stepped cautiously into the room and froze.

Meg rammed into my backside, almost knocking me off my feet.

My mouth must've been hanging open as my mother said, "Daryl Anne, you're gawking."

And why wouldn't I be? I hadn't heard her leave this morning.

And she wasn't alone. A man with a shock of white-blond hair stood at her side, towering over her. I scrambled to make sense of this. Had she gotten up before me and gone to breakfast with this guy—who'd recently installed our new security system? No, I realized. She was wearing the same thing she'd had on when she left for their date last night. Oh my God, was this a walk of shame? Oh, no, no, no. The thought sent another wave of unease through me. Mom was blushing as if she'd read my mind. As if she were guilty. Definitely not the behavior I expected from Susan Blessing, chaste widow.

But what behavior did I expect? She was an adult. Free to do whatever she wanted with whomever she wanted. I'd even encouraged her to start dating. But considering the dismay churning through me, I should've told her to take things slower. That, or I wasn't sure Whitey Grobowski was the right man for her. After all, how well did we know him?

Sure, he was nice enough looking for an older dude. He even seemed to make her happy, happier than she'd been since my dad passed away over a decade ago. I felt suddenly selfish and about eleven years old. She hadn't dated anyone in all those years. Not one date. Why would I wish that on her again? Did I want her to end up alone and lonely, her life centered on this shop and Gram and me? Without another shot at romantic love? No. But I had the feeling that she was going from zero to sixty in record time, and I feared she might get sucked into the dizzying whirl of that excitement. Might not listen to her heart or use good judgment. I'd rather see her put on the brakes, slow down. At least a bit.

Meg whispered in my ear, "I was going to ask how your mom's new relationship was going, but I see it's heatin' up."

I elbowed her as I took in Mom's attire. As I'd observed earlier, she still wore the burgundy A-line skirt and pale rose sweater set that I'd helped her select last night, along with the pearls Dad had given her the day they wed. Classic dinner and movie ensemble. Whitey had on navy twill pants and a matching long-sleeved shirt, the cuffs rolled up his muscled forearms. It was exactly the selection I would have chosen for him in my old position as Key Wardrobe for a Los Angeles–based TV sitcom. Perfect "working, blue-collar guy," right down to the company logo—GHSS, GIG HARBOR SECURITY SYSTEMS—over the pocket and the Leatherman tool secured to his belt loop.

"What have you two been up to this sunny morning?" Meg asked, the innocent note in her voice making me want to pinch her.

"We were just over at Something Old, Something New," Mom said, gesturing toward the shop across the street. "Bernice was showing off a new shipment of jewelry she picked up at an estate sale last week. There were a couple of really sweet antique bracelets and hairpieces. Oh, and she had an antique gold cake server set that she claimed was once owned by President Roosevelt's wife. It's solid gold with fancy carving and their initials engraved."

"It'd net somebody a pretty penny on eBay." Whitey gave a low whistle of appreciation, then shook his head. "That woman really should invest in better locks."

Mom huffed. "She should invest in one of your security systems, but don't take her rejecting that offer personally. There's no convincing Bernice. She's always been penny-wise and pound-foolish. Serve her right if she got robbed."

"Now, Susan, unruffle those feathers on my behalf," Whitey said softly. "I don't need her business as much as she might need mine, and I don't begrudge her the choice."

A rap on the glass door brought us all around. But butcher

paper prevented us from seeing who was there. Mom said, "Oh, that should be Jenny Carson, the temp I hired yesterday."

I knew she'd been interviewing for the position, of course. I just didn't realize she'd found and hired someone already. It was a relief, actually. Business quadrupled during the wedding expo, and seasonal helpers became a rare and priceless commodity.

"In that case," Whitey said, following Mom to the door, "I'll get out of your hair so you ladies can work. I've got my own appointment to get to down the street. I'll call you later, Susan."

Mom was beaming when she greeted Jenny, and Jenny seemed to think the smile was all for her. I could have told her different. Mom was smitten. Definitely falling for the first man she'd dated in fifteen years. This was a disaster. Hadn't anyone ever talked to her about the joys of playing the field? At least until she'd earned her dating cleats?

"Hi," Jenny said, glancing from Meg to me and back again as introductions were made, her honey-brown, slicked-back pony-tail switching like a metronome. She was tall, even in ballet shoes, but she was not ballerina thin. At around five-nine, she had the toned build of a gymnast. Her put-together appearance would immediately appeal to any potential employer.

"Jenny is planning her own wedding," Mom said.

Jenny nodded, then gushed in a voice that sounded younger than the twenty-two I'd guessed her to be. "Bradley's currently stationed in the Middle East. I'm not sure where. He can't say. We're getting married next Valentine's Day."

For Meg's sake, I winced inwardly at the new reminder that she was still single instead of enjoying the lavish honeymoon she'd planned. And I felt equally bad for Jenny. I couldn't imag-ine the fear of waking up every morning and not knowing for sure where your fiancé was or if he was okay. My mind flashed to

Seth Quinlan. Even though our relationship was only at the first date stage, I was grateful that his stint in the armed services was behind him.

In an effort to change the subject, and to see if Mom hadn't been influenced by appearance only, I said, "I haven't seen your resume, Jenny. Where did you work before?"

"The Veiled Bride in Portland. You've probably never heard of it."

But I had. "Actually we buy gowns from them occasionally."

"Really?" Her dark eyes rounded, and she laughed. "Why didn't I know that?"

"What brings you to this area?" Meg asked, echoing my own curiosity.

"Bradley's family lives in Gig Harbor. I'm staying with them while he's deployed." Jenny toyed with her right earring, a tiny red heart, as if it were hurting her earlobe.

"How long did you work for the Veiled Bride?" I asked, wondering about her actual experience.

"Daryl Anne, this is not a police interrogation," Mom said. "Jenny already has the job. Her references have been checked."

Wow. My mom putting me in my place in front of the hired help and my BFF. Not that I didn't deserve it. I did. Clearly.

"Sorry," I said, pondering why I felt the need to question my mother's judgment on this hire. I decided it was her judgment on the boyfriend front that I was questioning, but I couldn't do that verbally. Therefore I needed to stop taking out my frustration on the temp.

The door opened, and Hannah Farley, our other temp, scrambled inside, clutching a large shoulder bag to her chest as if to ward off anyone who might invade her private space. Whenever I looked at her, I had the impression of staring at a tropical beach—pale brown hair and eyebrows, white-sand complexion, and eyes the blue of tide pools. She offered a dour, "Morning."

Hannah was a cousin on my mother's side, younger than me by five years. She'd been a sneaky, sticky-fingered kid, always creeping up on me. I never heard her coming, didn't know she was there until I felt her breath on my neck. I hoped she'd out-grown that disturbing trait.

We all acknowledged her greeting. Mom, usually one to hug a relative, offered instead a warm smile. Hannah wasn't the touchy-feeling type.

Mom clapped her hands together as if to say, *Let's get this show rolling*. She told Hannah, "A new shipment is due any time this morning."

"'Kay," Hannah said, and took off for the back room.

She already knew the routine and her way around the shop. She'd worked the expos during the years I'd lived in Los Ange-les. Now that I was back, Gram and Mom had reassigned her to unpacking merchandise as it arrived, logging the items into the computer, and labeling them. Hannah would also be helping in alterations, her nimble fingers perfect for the delicate work that Gram could no longer do.

"Daryl Anne, Jenny and I will finish up the categorizing in the showroom," Mom said. "You and Meg should really start putting those display cases together."

"Yay," Meg said as soon as we were alone in the salon. "I'd rather do something artistic. That left-brain stuff gives me a migraine."

I chuckled. Meg can do magic with makeup and hair. She excels at creative. I have an eye for detail and overall composition.

"Do we have a theme?"

"Yes, 'buy this dress.'"

We laughed and got to work. Since the shop sold dresses that ran the gambit from sample sizes to real women sizes, the mannequins reflected that. I was jacking up my last "bride"—adding a veil, tiara, and jewelry—when noise from outside caught my attention. I crept to the glass and tore a peephole in the paper.

Meg apparently hadn't heard the sound. Probably because she was still wrestling her mannequin into a wedding gown. She was much better with a makeup brush and likely wished that was what she was doing instead. But I gave her points for not complaining. "Daryl Anne, what are you doing? We haven't finished this display yet. I thought you didn't want anyone peeping in before the big reveal."

"No one's paying the least attention to what I'm doing. It's Something Old, Something New that's drawing gawkers like seagulls to fish guts," I said, eyeing the cop car parking at the curb outside the store across the street.

"Considering the markup on Bernice's antiques"—Meg grunted as she worked the corset closed on the gown—"a shopper probably collapsed after looking at a price tag."

"In that case, Bernice would've sent for an ambulance, not the police," I said, glancing at her over my shoulder. I recalled Mom saying, *"Serve her right if she got robbed."*

"The police?" Meg's head popped up, but she seemed not to care why the cops were at Something Old, Something New. "Sheriff Gooden or Troy?"

Troy was Troy O'Malley, Meg's junior and high school sweetheart, the man everyone thought she'd marry. Once upon a time. Until beauty college and the navy intervened.

But from the dreamy tone she'd just used to say his name, I figured she might be falling back in love with him. Or maybe—as I'd suspected a couple of months ago—she'd never really gotten over him. "It was Troy."

Meg set aside the mannequin, untangled herself from the voluminous satin skirt of the Vera Wang gown, and picked through the display to stand by my side. "Is he coming here?"

"No." I shook my head. "He went into Bernice's store."

"Bernice's?" she said, sounding disappointed.

I frowned. Had she paid no attention to what I'd been saying? I started to ask, but the look in her eyes stopped me. She gave a toss of her hair, a sign that she had a bee in her bonnet. "Do you think I'm dumb for even considering starting up a relationship with him again?"

I studied her. "Have you started up with him again?"

"Not officially. Maybe not at all. I mean, when I was unavailable, he couldn't stop telling me that we belonged together, but since my engagement ended, well, it's like he's avoiding me."

I hated the hurt in her voice, but lately that emotion seemed to keep popping up. Life had been anything but kind. I offered her an understanding smile. "Troy said he was going to give you space and time…remember? You're dealing with the loss of your mom and the whole mess with Peter. Troy doesn't want to pressure you."

She arched a skeptic brow. "But it was okay to pressure me when I was hours away from exchanging vows with someone else?"

She had a point, but still, I rolled my eyes, knowing I'd just been presented with a peek into my best friend's mind, a glimpse at what I call the Chaotic Express. Meg wanted it both ways, but mostly she wanted it her way. If only she could decide what that was. "Do you want a relationship with him or not?"

"What if he only wanted me because he thought someone else wanted me?"

"I don't think that was the case."

"Then why didn't he come to see me? I told him I was helping you in the shop today."

"Meg, Troy was wearing his uniform." I turned back to the window. "He's working."

"Working?" It seemed to take a second for that to register. Her eyes widened. "What do you mean? What's going on?"

Sure, now she's curious.

The next second she was beside me, trying to see through the slit in the butcher paper. "Has he come out yet?"

"Nope." I stepped aside, sharing my sliver of street view.

"There's a lot of people gathering out there." She glanced up at me, eyes ripe with speculation. "Do you think Bernice was robbed?"

"Maybe…"

"I'm going to find out." She turned and began picking her way out of the window display with me right behind her.

As soon as I unlocked and opened the door, Meg rushed out ahead of me. The crowd had grown and spilled into the street, their colliding voices sounding like a discordant choir practicing hymns off-key. I couldn't make out what anyone was saying. Meg headed into the thick of things. I hung back, a bad feeling freezing my feet to the spot. My gaze zeroed in on Something Old, Something New, which inhabited a Victorian three-story house that had been built by one of the founding fathers of Weddingville, Bernice's great-great-great-uncle.

A siren bleated like a sheep with hiccups, clearing a path for a second police car to make its way to the shop. My heart began to pound. Hard. One cop car was interesting but not usually anything to get too excited about. Two cop cars screamed "real crime." The last time anything this official occurred, there'd been a murder.

Troy emerged from the building, waving people back. A cap covered his blue-black hair but not his piercing blue eyes, which were scanning the onlookers. He glanced past Meg and me. His cold gaze sent a shiver down my spine, and I retreated several feet. Oh, crap. I hadn't shut or locked the bridal shop door. As I spun around to do that, I was nearly run over by Whitey.

His face was as pale as his hair. He was panting. His eyes were wild as though something or someone were after him. "I need to get inside, Daryl Anne. Now."

"There he is!" Bernice's voice ripped through the air, silencing the crowd. I spun toward Something Old, Something New. She was tugging on Troy's sleeve, her gray hair as frenzied as a disturbed beehive, her arm outstretched. The crowd gasped and parted like a split seam. Shock shot through me. Bernice was pointing at Whitey. "That's him! He's the one who stole President Roosevelt's cake server set!"

Chapter 2

I stepped back. Whitey looked more frantic than ever. Then Bernice shouted her accusation again, pushed past Troy, and came running through the parted crowd like an ostrich in a ravine. Troy charged after her. The crowd cheered encouragement. Whitey blanched, bumped by me, and shoved into the bridal shop. Troy gained on a panting Bernice, overtaking her by six feet. He arrived just as the door was shut in my face.

He cursed under his breath, then glanced at me and apologized for swearing. "Do you have the key, Daryl Anne?"

I did, but I hadn't heard the lock click. I reached for the handle. The door opened, and Troy rushed in. I could see Whitey in there, too. Along with my mother. Bernice grabbed my arm. "Outta my way, Daryl Anne."

The crowd surged toward us. Holy cow. We were going to be trampled.

"No!" Fear gave me the strength to free myself from the irate owner of Something Old, Something New. I shoved her toward the charging mob, ducked into the bridal shop, and twisted the lock.

I slumped into the door, my breath lodged in my throat. Loud voices, Bernice's the only distinguishable one, railed against the glass at my back. My knees wobbled as if I were holding a tornado at bay. My gaze locked on the scene in the salon.

Coming into the bridal shop is like entering a church. A feeling of reverence or high joy fills you. For this is where the true commitment to marriage is made—not at the time of the proposal, not the putting on of the engagement ring but by taking the most important step any bride-to-be can. Selecting her gown. She knows only then that there is no turning back. She will mean every word of the vows that she speaks on that special day, will dedicate her heart and her life to the love she feels for her chosen mate.

But what was going on in here now washed away the magic from this place of pristine gowns and exalted hope, leaving in its wake a sinister tension. The commotion had brought my mother from the storeroom. She'd halted halfway into the salon, apparently stunned, like me, into silence.

Troy had Whitey spread-eagled against a wall like a common thug, patting him down.

I felt a breath on my neck and nearly jumped out of my skin when I realized Hannah was beside me. "There's just something about a man in uniform...," she whispered, her gaze locked on Troy.

"What do you think you're doing, Officer O'Malley?" Mom demanded, using the voice she saved for particularly difficult customers. "What is the meaning of this?"

"Please stay where you are, Ms. Blessing," Troy said, holding his palm toward her like a human stop sign. "I'm just doing my duty."

"What duty?" Mom demanded, ignoring the warning to stay put as she started toward the two men. From the fierce glint in her eyes, I wasn't sure what exactly she intended to do, but I feared it might land her in handcuffs.

I jumped in, hoping to divert her. "Bernice's store was robbed, Mom. She claims Whitey stole the Roosevelt wedding server set."

"What?" Whitey said, jerking to look over his shoulder. "I did not."

"Then why'd you run?" Troy demanded, stepping back and tugging the other man around.

Whitey squirmed, wiggling his legs as if adjusting himself as discreetly as possible. His neck had a reddish hue, a sign that he was either embarrassed at being felt up by another man or annoyed. Maybe both. He kept his gaze steadied on Troy. "I don't know what you mean."

I remembered the wild look of desperation on his face when he'd insisted I let him into the bridal shop. He probably had a perfectly innocent reason for that. One he'd explain right now. Right?

"It seemed like you were running from me," Troy said.

Whitey looked as if he'd like to tell the cop to have his eyes checked. He shook his head. "Wasn't."

Keep out of it, Daryl Anne. Mom will be ticked if you say anything that will put her boyfriend into hotter water than he's already in. Why couldn't I ever listen to the good advice that little voice in my head offered? I blurted out, "You seemed like you wanted to get away from something."

"Daryl Anne," Mom gasped, scowling at me. She was wringing her hands. "That's nonsense. Whitey was just coming back to keep our lunch date. Weren't you, Whitey? Tell them."

"Tattletale," Hannah whispered near my shoulder. I wanted to bat her away like an annoying fly.

Whitey sighed. He lifted his head and glanced at Mom with

regret. "Daryl Anne's right, Susan. I was trying to get away from someone. Three someones, actually. Your mother-in-law's Bunco club."

"What?" Mom frowned. "Why?"

Troy shuffled his feet, his boots clunking on the hardwood beneath his heels. Whitey returned his focus to the cop. Troy moved back, putting more space between himself and his suspect. He withdrew a pencil and a small, ringed tablet from his shirt pocket. "Why don't you just explain that, Mr. Grobowski?"

Whitey tucked in a loose shirttail and adjusted the baseball cap on his snowy hair. "I had an appointment this morning with Wanda Perroni, the owner of the Wedding Cakery."

"That's right, Troy," Mom said. "I asked him to bring back some of Wanda's cannoli."

"I forgot that, Susan. I'm sorry," Whitey said.

A pang of regret swept through me. Wanda baked the freshest cakes and sweetest pastries this side of heaven, and despite the seriousness of the moment, my mouth began to water at the thought of some cannoli.

"Are you in need of a wedding cake, Mr. Brokowski?" Troy asked, frowning.

"No." Whitey answered too quickly, wincing as if Troy had pinched him. He swallowed, his Adam's apple bobbing. "No. Mrs. Perroni expressed an interest in obtaining one of my security systems."

"And...," Troy said when Whitey didn't continue.

"And when I arrived, she wasn't alone," Whitey said, as if reliving the memory were a physical pain. I swear if his shirt had been buttoned at the neck, he would've tugged at it. "She'd invited two friends—Velda Weeks and Jeanette Corn—to sit in on the meeting."

I groaned internally. Wanda, Velda, and Jeanette. I'd suffered a few run-ins with that senior, tongue-wagging trio.

Whitey cleared his throat. "They claimed to also be interested in my security systems. I figured it was about to be a very profitable morning."

"But it wasn't?" Troy asked, his voice as neutral as Switzerland.

Whitey twisted his mouth. "Let's just say it didn't go exactly as planned."

Troy jotted something in his tablet. I wasn't sure what he was writing, but as far as I could tell, Whitey hadn't said anything that Troy might soon forget.

Mom said, "So, what happened?"

Whitey shook his head as if still not believing what had gone down. "I presented my sales pitch along with brochures that detail exactly which options or equipment comes with my four different packages. You can look in my briefcase. Oh, hell, I left my briefcase at the bakery."

"The brochures list all of his prices," Mom informed Troy.

Troy nodded. "Yeah, I figured. But what does any of this have to do with the robbery, Mr. Brokowski?"

"Nothing," Whitey said, seeming about to blow his top. "I didn't rob that store."

I wanted to believe him as much as my mother did, but he was acting guilty of something.

"I'd like to believe you, but surely you realize by running you look guilty." Troy's calm was unnerving.

"I had to run," Whitey said, his voice full of frustration. "Those Bunco women were chasing me."

Troy stayed mute, studying Whitey. The silence stretched out until Whitey lost it. "I didn't rob anyone."

"Of course you didn't." Mom leaped to his defense, as if she'd been at his side all morning and knew for a fact that he was completely innocent.

I, on the other hand, couldn't stop wondering why he kept fidgeting. If he was innocent, why didn't he answer the most important question? "*Why* were the women chasing you?"

Whitey glanced in my direction, as though seeing me for the first time. He blinked, then seemed to realize I might be giving him the benefit of the doubt, and he grabbed on to it like a lifeline. Any port in a storm. "Like I said, I thought they were interested in buying, or at least considering, one of my security systems. But I quickly understood that they were more interested in finding out about…me."

I swear Troy's ears twitched. "What about you?"

"I don't know…" Whitey rubbed his hands on his pants.

"A blind person can see he's lying," Hannah whispered.

"Don't you have a shipment to unpack?" I whispered back.

"It's not going anywhere," she countered.

"Please, just tell the man," Mom implored Whitey, a quiver in her voice. Was she losing trust in her beau, or was she afraid Troy would haul him to jail? My heart squeezed. It wasn't like she didn't have reason to imagine such a scenario after her own ordeal with the local police when Meg's mom was killed.

"They wanted to know—" Whitey broke off and looked away, his neck getting redder. His gaze fixed on the gown Meg had abandoned on the floor near the display window. "They wanted to know if my intentions were honorable…you know, about you."

Seriously? They'd appointed themselves the love police? I stifled a laugh, but Mom gasped. "Why those nosy old biddies…"

"What prompted them to chase after you?" Troy said.

Whitey swallowed hard. "The more personal the question got,

the more uncomfortable I got. I realized the so-called meeting was just a ploy. None of those women wanted a security system. So I thanked them for their time and consideration and excused myself. I'd made the mistake of walking there. I was halfway back here when I heard them calling my name. Shouting questions at me in the street. I picked up my pace, but the sidewalks were crowded, and damn, those old broads are fast. People started to stop and stare, until all I could think was to get away."

"O'Malley!" A loud knock sounded on the door. "You in there?"

"It's Sheriff Gooden," Hannah said, disappearing a second later like a wisp of smoke.

I hurried back to the door, wishing I had access here to the monitors Whitey had installed in the office and our living quarters that allowed us to see who stood outside the door. Before unlocking the latch, I asked, "Are you alone, Sheriff?"

"Daryl Anne Blessing, you let me in there right now. This is official WPD business. A crime has been committed." I remembered how cold this man could be when it came to his duty. I appreciated his dedication to the law and safety of those he was entrusted to protect but still didn't think he was much of a detective. Solving crimes took a clever man. Sheriff Gooden was just a good, honest policeman elected by the majority for his ability as a mediator.

I eased the door open and peered into his squinting eyes, his lined face. He was in his forties but could pass for sixty. To my relief, most of the crowd had dispersed. Except for Bernice. She hovered behind the sheriff.

I pointed at Bernice. "I'm not letting her in."

He nodded. "Bernice, go back to your store."

"But—"

"Allow me to do my job." His voice was low and full of authority.

"All right," she said begrudgingly, "but don't let that snake oil salesman pull the wool over your eyes."

My narrowed gaze caused Bernice to retreat a step, but her expression remained adamant. "I'm sorry, Daryl Anne, but your mother's being taken in by that slick talker. The whole town thinks so."

The whole town? Since when had she become the spokesperson for the whole town? It took every bit of willpower I possessed not to verbally cut her to shreds. Sometimes it's better to hold your tongue than to have the last word. I closed the door. If the gossips hadn't already been spouting opinions about Mom dating a man who was not a hometown resident, they would be after this morning. Thanks to the love police and Bernice.

And since Sheriff Gooden insisted on hauling Whitey to the station for further questioning, I feared too many of those opinions would slant in Bernice's favor.

* * *

Later, as I stood outside checking the display window, I caught a reflection in the glass that caused my heart to skip. I'd never been so glad to see Seth Quinlan, the owner of Cherished Moments photo studio, striding across the street toward me. The chill around my heart began to melt. He wasn't pretty-boy handsome, like David Beckham or Brad Pitt, but his rugged features, crooked grin, and warm chocolate eyes added up to one stunningly sexy male.

He was coming from Something Old, Something New, a camera slung around his neck, another attached to his hip. The police hired him to shoot crime scenes on those few occasions that a crime was committed in Weddingville, and that was likely what he'd been doing at Bernice's.

As he neared, he seemed to read the distress I couldn't hide. He frowned, then grinned, and I knew he was contemplating how to lift my spirits. "A nickel for your thoughts, Blessing," Seth said, an inside joke between us.

"A nickel, Quinlan?" I tilted my head, gazing up at him. His usual offer was the old one-cent standard.

"Yeah." He shoved his fingers through his thick tawny hair, reconfiguring it as a gust of wind might do. "A nickel."

I arched a brow, curious. "Why so much?"

He leaned in, his sandalwood scent filling me. "Since I've gotten to know you, I've realized your thoughts are worth more than a mere penny."

I wasn't in the mood to smile but darned if I didn't. A small one. He just had a way of untwisting the knot in my stomach like nothing else could. Unfortunately, the sensation was fleeting. As soon as I dragged him into the bridal shop, closing the door behind us and glancing at my mother, the gut-wrench returned.

Seth stayed by the door as I hurried to her side, sinking next to her on the red velvet love seat. Distress wafted off her like dust motes in the dimmed light. I took her hands. "I thought you'd gone upstairs to lie down."

"I can't."

"Mom, it'll be okay. They haven't arrested Whitey. They're just questioning him."

"That's not reassuring, Daryl Anne," Mom said. "You know how narrow-minded Sheriff Gooden can be. They're probably strip-searching Whitey right now."

My mouth fell open at the suggestion, even as I realized

why she must've said it. I wanted to throw up. "Did they strip-search you?"

Her face flushed to a shade of hot pink, and she visibly shuddered.

I closed my eyes against images of the humiliation this gentle, proper woman had endured while she'd been incarcerated, charged with murdering Meg's mother. But I couldn't quell the nausea.

A cough of someone clearing their throat caught my attention. I glanced toward the storeroom door and spied my paternal grandmother, Wilhelmina Blessing—known to one and all as Billie—standing there. Tall and reed thin, dressed in vintage Chanel, she wore her black hair twisted into a chignon. She was scowling, her lips pursed, and I could see trouble brewing in those blue eyes that were so like my own.

Apparently Seth caught it, too. "It's procedure," he said, striding toward the love seat. He kept his voice soft as though to absorb some of the shock and dismay lingering like a noxious cloud in the room. "But it's only done if you're placed under arrest."

Maybe Mom would listen to him, if not to me. After all, Seth wasn't just friends with Troy; they also shared a working relationship. He knew a little about law enforcement stuff.

"See, Mom. Seth agrees. The police are only questioning Whitey."

"Seth, weren't you called in to take photos at Bernice's?" Billie asked.

"Yes," Seth admitted.

"Well, then maybe you caught something on film that will lead to the real culprit," Billie said.

Seth shook his head. "I'm not allowed to discuss the actual investigation with anyone at this point, Billie."

Mom pleaded with her gaze. "Sheriff Gooden even checked my purse, as if that cake serving set would fit into my clutch."

"They'll check Whitey's van and his briefcase, too, Mom."

"They won't find anything. He didn't take it. It was on the counter when we left that wretched shop. I'll swear to that."

"What did you photograph at Bernice's?" I asked Seth. "A bare countertop?"

"I can't say." He gave me a you-know-better-than-to-ask look.

"She should've put something that valuable in a locked display case," Billie said.

Mom scrunched her face as if she might spit. "What Bernice should've done was hired Whitey to add security cameras. Instead, in front of the whole town, mind you, she accuses him of ripping her off!"

The whole town again? Wow. I'd only seen my usually mild-mannered mother this close to losing it once before, and I didn't relish a repeat, but my tongue felt glued to the roof of my mouth, leaving me unable to speak.

"I'll never buy another thing from that woman. I'll have her Bunco card revoked." Gram could quell a bridezilla with that raised eyebrow.

"Is there such a thing as a Bunco card?" Jenny asked, startling me. My mouth dried. I hadn't seen her standing in the shadows behind Gram. Was Hannah lurking nearby, too? Probably. But I was more concerned about Jenny. This was hardly the first-day impression to be giving a new employee. She had a deer-in-the-headlights glaze to her eyes while her body seemed ready for flight. *Probably wondering if she's made a major error taking a job with the obviously insane Blessing family.* If she quit, we'd be hard pressed to find a replacement on such short notice.

On the other hand, adversity proved mettle. If Jenny fled, then she wouldn't have been able to handle the wedding expo either. We needed an assistant with backbone and pluck. Someone who could take whatever came her way and handle it with poise.

Gram didn't answer the Bunco card question. She started toward the door, her face set. "I'm going to give that Bernice a piece of my mind. Right now."

"No." I hurried after her, catching her at the door. I impulsively grabbed for her arm but caught her injured wrist by mistake. She yelped, but stopped. She'd cracked the same bone twice in two months, and it wasn't healing as quickly as the first time. "Oh my God, Gram, I'm sorry. Did I hurt you?"

"Nothing like the hurt I'm going to put on Bernice."

Chapter 3

W hat happened to innocent until proven guilty?" I asked Meg as we finished our morning run and approached the source of our after-jog reward.

Meg tugged off the scrunchie holding her mass of curls at bay. She gave a shake of her head. Her hair tumbled free around her shoulders, catching glints of sunlight in its fiery strands. "Social media killed it."

"Really?" I toweled my forehead. The only thing glinting on me was sweat. "On what do you base your conclusion—?"

"Observation. Haven't you noticed that everyone seems to think their opinion about a crime is what happened rather than what the actual evidence proves? They don't give a fig about the damage their careless speculation does to the often-innocent, accused individual and his or her family."

I could attest to that, having been through it when my mom was in jail. "Bernice doesn't have one bit of proof against Whitey, but she's got tongues wagging like red flags in a high wind. Mom is beside herself, and Billie is plotting revenge." I was no better off. Running four miles this morning hadn't unfurled the knot of anger inside me.

Meg patted my back. "Be thankful Blessing's Bridal doesn't rely on locals to sustain its income. Unlike this espresso stand."

"Huh?"

"My point is that a small business like this could be damaged if nasty rumors were flying around about its proprietor. Locals might shun this coffee shop, whereas you don't have to rely on locals to sustain your income."

"I am grateful that gossip won't hurt our bottom line, but I don't like knowing friends and neighbors are making quick judgments based on the skewed accusations of one woman. How do you defend that?"

"You don't. You ignore it."

But what if Bernice was right? What if Whitey had taken the cake server set? What do we really know about him? I couldn't bring myself to say that out loud. Not even to Meg. It just felt too disloyal to Mom.

"I can't believe anyone would treat your family badly. If not for the bridal shop, this place would be a ghost town," Meg declared, digging into the coin pouch built into her jogging pants.

Meg was dead serious, but her fierce loyalty warmed my heart. I laughed. "You make it sound like we were EMTs resurrecting a drowning victim."

"You were."

"Like death and taxes, weddings will occur," I said. "That is what kept us afloat when those around us were sinking. The city council took note and made some smart choices."

"Turning this town into a one-stop wedding site was brilliant, yes, but if not for Blessing's Bridal, that inspired idea wouldn't likely have popped into anyone's head."

She was right. Renaming the stores and gearing merchandise toward all things bridal had saved this town. My gaze zeroed in on the espresso shop. The proprietor, Priscilla Pressley, was a rabid Elvis fan. Her house and shop were filled with Elvis memorabilia. Two husbands had run off because she was more in love with the deceased icon than with them.

Meg leaned in. "If Priscilla's current boyfriend were accused of a crime, Pre-Wedding Jitters would be singing 'Heartbreak Hotel.'"

Instead, what issued from the speakers of the latte stand was Elvis crooning "Suspicious Minds," mocking me. I cringed and considered skipping the grande caramel macchiato I'd been anticipating. But Meg dragged me through the door. The interior was smaller than the average Starbucks, the seating limited to four cocktail-sized tables, all of them, thankfully, empty at the moment.

My mouth watered at the rush of rich aromas filling my senses. I love coffee. Not that I've tried every variety offered here, but I'm working on it. Just not today. I followed Meg to the counter and listened to her order. Maybe it was my mood, or maybe I was being paranoid, but I felt like someone was staring at me. When I glanced over my shoulder, I came eye to eye with a life-sized cutout of Elvis Presley. Everywhere I looked... Elvis.

I whispered to my best friend, "A more appropriate name for this place would've been Graceland."

Meg stifled a laugh. "Priscilla probably considered that but didn't want to get sued. Besides, that name doesn't have a wedding connection that the city council would've approved."

I smiled at the barista. Not Priscilla, but her daughter, named Lisa Marie, of course. She had attitude and a fresh mouth, was twenty, pretty, and knew it. She and Meg exchanged a look of empathy, a bond that had formed between them when Lisa Marie's fiancé dumped her a while back for the daughter of his rich boss.

Lisa Marie seemed to have put heartbreak behind her faster

than Meg. But then she hadn't also lost her mother. She said, "Daryl Anne, I'm sorry about the rumors flying around. I don't believe them for a minute. Especially after talking to the new temp at SOSN this morning and getting the real scoop."

"SOSN?" Meg asked.

"Something Old, Something New," I said. "What scoop, Lisa Marie?"

Lisa Marie started our drinks, speaking louder to be heard over the grinding of the coffee beans. "Apparently, Bernice wasn't even in the main area of the shop when the Roosevelt cake server set went missing. A sudden influx of customers crowded into the store as soon as Bernice had disappeared into the back room to deal with a recent delivery. The new girl had been about to place the set your mom and her beau had been looking at into the safe. She got distracted and forgot. When she remembered, the cake server set had vanished."

"Did she tell the police?" Meg asked.

Lisa Marie shook her head as she worked her magic with the espresso machine. It began to hiss and steam. "She's afraid she'll lose her job, and she really needs the work."

I didn't want to, but I felt sorry for the girl. Considering how vehemently Bernice had come after Whitey, she would surely fire the young woman. My sympathy, however, didn't extend to having someone else arrested for a crime they didn't commit or having their reputation destroyed by false accusations. "She must come forward."

"I'm working on her to fess up. If not to Bernice, then to Sheriff Gooden."

I agreed. Her silence wasn't helping Whitey.

"I told her shit happens," Lisa Marie said. "We all deal with sticky-fingered customers. That's what insurance is for. It even happens here. Someone jacked an Elvis and Priscilla mug recently. Not sure exactly when, but Mom noticed right off."

Probably mislaid it, I thought. Priscilla wasn't exactly the roundest CD in the jukebox.

Lisa Marie handed me my drink. "It was only a ten-dollar mug. Not worth submitting to insurance. Cost of doing business sometimes."

"Where is your mom, by the way?" Meg stuck a straw through the lid of her espresso cup.

Lisa Marie rolled her eyes. "Off with the King Sisters. That's her Elvis sisterhood. Somewhere in Reno investigating the latest Elvis sighting."

Grinning, we headed to one of the empty tables just as three young women rushed in. Two of them were laughing and chatting; the third was head down, eyes on her cell phone. They placed their orders and retreated to a nearby table.

Meg and I were still chuckling over Priscilla and her sisterhood on their fruitless hunt. Meg said, "Long live the king."

My phone vibrated. "Ah, it's a text from Seth."

Meg smiled. "I like that man."

"Me too." I read the text. "Hey, did you know about this? Your dad is fixing dinner for Mom, Whitey, Gram, and me at the café tonight. Apparently Seth is invited, too."

"Oh no, I forgot to tell you. Dad will shoot me. He's so pissed at how people are reacting to Bernice's accusation that he wants your mom and Billie to know he doesn't believe it for a minute. Please say you don't have plans already."

"Are you kidding?" I somehow managed to say over the lump of gratitude in my throat. The best gifts didn't always come wrapped with ribbons and bows, I realized, but were more precious than anything money could buy. "We'll be there."

"Six sharp. He's shutting the café down for the night to do this."

I smiled, noticing how my espresso tasted even better than it had a second ago.

A sudden outcry from the other table startled me. "Oh my God," one of the young women said. "According to TMZ, Peter Wolfe has eloped with his new assistant."

Sighs of regret followed the announcement.

I jerked my gaze to Meg, distress flooding my veins. She looked stricken. I reached for her hand. "It's probably not even true."

"I don't have my phone," Meg said, patting herself down. Unlike most of our friends, she'd grown up without electronic devices. Big Finn wanted his daughter to stay connected with people in person and not through a screen. So Meg never considered her cell an extension of herself. She could take it or leave it. Mostly, she mislaid it. "Google it on yours."

I pulled up the TMZ website, and there it was. Top of the newsfeed. *International star Peter Wolfe eloped today with his new personal assistant, Ash Moon.* Peter was the actor Meg had almost married eight weeks earlier. Ash was Meg's former makeup artist assistant on the sitcom we'd worked for in Los Angeles, now Peter's new assistant.

"Wasn't Peter Wolfe engaged to marry someone else a couple of months ago?" asked another of the women at the next table. "Someone who used to live around here?"

Meg stumbled to her feet and rushed out the door. I hurried after her, but when I got outside, she was gone.

* * *

I worried about Meg all afternoon as I attended to giddy brides-to-be and juggled their opinionated entourages. She wasn't answering her phone or my text messages. Not that this was of real concern. Meg might have just not found her phone yet.

I kept telling myself that as I peered into my closet trying to decide what to wear to dinner. I'd learned my sense of style from my grandmother. My wardrobe consisted of classic pieces at its foundation, which I updated with trendy accessories. Tonight was a balmy seventy-five. I slipped into some espadrilles and reached for a DVF wrap dress with a summery pattern of pinks and reds. I'd picked it up in a favorite Los Angeles consignment shop where there were racks of designer discards culled from rich Hollywood wives and sold at knockoff prices. I missed that shop.

"Wow," Seth responded when he showed up to walk me to the café. "I like."

"I'm glad. I wore it for you." I strove to keep my voice light, but Seth was too sharp. He picked up on my stressful mood.

I turned to shut and lock the back door of the bridal shop, and Seth leaned over me and whispered in my ear, "If I could take away the worry lines around your beautiful mouth, Blessing, I'd do it in a heartbeat."

I shifted around, gazing first at his sexy lips and then into his eyes, melting at the affection that greeted me. "How exactly would you do that, Quinlan?"

"Any way you want me to. Use your imagination." He traced a finger from my temple to my chin, a crooked smile softening his sharp features and sending tendrils of need soaring through me.

"I have a vivid imagination," I warned, my voice breathy with desire.

"I'm counting on that. But right now, we're expected elsewhere."

I was glad traffic had died down to around twenty or so cars and that the crowded sidewalks of earlier were now passable. Seth took my hand then, right there on Front Street, where anyone passing by or looking out a window could see. *Let the gossipy imaginations run wild*. I didn't care. His touch was warm, his grip possessive yet tender, and my hand seemed small and delicate against his palm. My pulse danced. If just holding his hand made me feel this much better, I might die a joyous death while receiving his full-on, stress-releasing treatment.

I struggled to regain my composure. "Mom, Whitey, and Gram left about ten minutes ago."

He picked up our pace. "I don't like being the last one to a party."

A group of shoppers flowed around us like salmon swimming upstream.

"Party? Is that what you call dinner with friends?"

"Any time with you is a party."

I smirked, shaking my head. "Okay, you win."

"Good. I like winning." He leaned toward me, his breath feathery on my cheek. "And I love nights like this. It feels like there's magic in the air. Do you feel it, Blessing?"

I glanced at the blue sky, listened to the seagulls crying, and smelled the salty air. It was a magical place to be sure, but no matter how much I wanted to lose myself in romantic suggestions and fantasies, my mind kept returning to Meg. "I suppose…"

"You suppose?"

I sighed. "I'm worried about Meg."

"Oh, I think she'll be fine."

"Fine? How can you say that?" He hadn't seen her reaction that morning to the news about Peter and Ash. I stopped in my tracks as something occurred to me. "You did hear the news, right?"

"What news?" He seemed overly cautious, not like someone about to be told something they didn't know, but like someone afraid of giving out information that he shouldn't be offering.

I plunged on despite that strangeness. "Peter Wolfe eloped this afternoon with Meg's former assistant, Ash Moon."

His expression relaxed. "Oh, sure, I heard. But you say that like Meg not marrying Wolfe was a mistake."

"No, no. It's not that. As far as I'm concerned, Meg dodged a bullet two months ago. But she was hit with some hard life lessons, and I'm not convinced she's come to terms with it all. I mean, it would be a lot for a mentally grounded person to work through. Whereas Meg usually runs with her heart." Often to her detriment.

"Is that such a bad thing?"

"No." In fact, one of the things I loved about Meg was her spontaneity. Or maybe it was a trait I envied, rather than loved, since I tended too much toward caution. I explained to Seth how we'd learned of the elopement. "It's just that, after she found out, she took off, and I haven't been able to reach her since this morning."

He considered that, then shrugged. "If it was anyone else, then maybe you'd have reason to worry, but Meg is always losing her phone."

"Yeah, I thought of that, too. I hope that's it."

"You can ask her yourself in a few seconds."

We'd arrived at Cold Feet Café, the diner owned by Meg's father, Big Finn Reilly, and his new wife, Zelda Love, the town's resident wedding planner. A sign hung in the window that read CLOSED FOR PRIVATE PARTY. The blinds were drawn, but music escaped from within along with muted chatter and the aroma of something delicious.

Seth rapped three times; then the door swung open, and Troy stood there, grinning. He was as handsome in civvies as he was in uniform, especially tonight in a polo shirt the color of the sky and gray chinos, his face tanned, his blue-black hair untamed. But for some reason, he didn't get my juices flowing like one glance from Seth always did. Maybe I wasn't into pretty boys. Or maybe it was because he'd been Meg's for as far back as I could recall and therefore eternally "off-limits."

"Cutting it close, aren't you?" he said more to Seth than to me.

I puzzled at the exchange but figured maybe Big Finn was getting impatient about the meal he'd prepared for everyone. We were ushered inside. The interior resembled a '50s style diner, black-and-white checkered flooring, a long counter with built-in swivel stools, and booths along the outside wall. The views were of the water and dock areas. I glanced at the familiar faces, pleasantly surprised to note that Troy's parents were here as well.

Zelda was perched on one of the stools, looking like "hostess at a beach party" with her crayon-yellow hair, white capri pants, and rainbow-colored chiffon top. Big Finn sat next to her and brought to mind a redheaded Brando in *On the Waterfront*, black T-shirt and jeans rolled at the cuffs.

"Isn't this exciting?" asked Gwen O'Malley. If I were casting Troy's mother in a movie, Audrey Hepburn would win the role. Gwen had a similar lithe ballerina's body and wore her dark brown hair slicked off her high forehead in a simple knot. If only she didn't dress like a Bedazzled Barbie.

She offered me a plastic champagne glass filled with clear bubbly liquid, then gave Seth one, too. I lifted a brow and said to Seth, "Champagne? Tell me we're celebrating the capture of the cake server thief and that the purloined item is in evidence or has been returned to Bernice."

Seth grinned. "Something even better."

Troy's mother sighed. "A gazillion times better."

Troy's dad, Joe O'Malley, had joined my family standing

around the counter and was chatting with Whitey. Except for the color of his eyes, Troy was a younger version of his old man.

"Don't you love impromptu things?" Gwen said. "Although I suppose this can't actually be called impromptu given their history."

I swallowed the urge to ask what the hell she was talking about, but then Meg appeared from around the far end counter, coming toward me. Everyone had stepped aside as if to clear an aisle for her in the center of the café. I started toward her, anxious to see how she was doing. But Troy gestured me back and went in my place. Seth pulled me to his side, holding my hand again, making me light-headed. Or maybe it was the champagne.

Meg watched Troy, her expression uncertain, leery. "What are you doing?"

Troy cleared his throat and caught her hands. "Meg, sometimes a man doesn't know what he wants or needs until he looks around and realizes that he had it once but let it slip away."

Joe O'Malley said, "Sometimes a man is a dumbshit."

Everyone laughed.

Troy shot his dad a keep-your-yap-shut-you're-interrupting-my -moment look and then gave his full attention to Meg. "I lost you once when I shipped out. I almost lost you a second time two months ago. And since third time's the charm, I'm not going to risk it happening again. I've always wanted you to have so much more than I can ever give, but I'm older and wiser now. I don't have riches, but I can offer you a lifetime of love."

He went down on one knee. Meg gasped. Her cheeks grew pink. "I did it right this time, Meg. I asked your dad for his blessing, and he gave it. So what do you say? Will you do me the honor of becoming my wife?"

He presented a ring, a ruby center stone with white diamonds circling it. "It was Granny O'Malley's engagement ring. She left it to me to give to my bride, but if you don't like it, I'll get you whatever you want."

The room held its breath as we all awaited Meg's answer. I thought she might run.

"I love you more than life itself," Troy said. "I always have, and I always will."

Meg still didn't speak, but she began nodding, tears splashing from her eyes. Troy slipped the ring onto her finger and rose, shouting a cheer. He lifted Meg to him and soundly kissed her.

Everyone began applauding and hooting, offering congratulations. Laughing. Crying. I stood there stunned. I couldn't stop thinking about this happening on the same day that Meg's ex eloped. Was this a reaction to that? Or was Meg really ready to trust Troy again and take this next step in their relationship?

A bad feeling slipped through the excitement in the room and twined itself around my heart. I should be happy for Meg and Troy. Not worried. I gulped the rest of my champagne, praying I hadn't tossed out my maid-of-honor handbook.

Chapter 4

The next day, Velda Weeks, Jeanette Corn, and Wanda Perroni, the gossip trio from hell, caught me on my way to collect Meg for our morning jog. I hadn't slept much the night before and was distracted by the crisp, sunny morning, the sweet, trilling birdsong, the thick salty air, and of course, my ongoing concern for my best friend's emotional well-being. Otherwise, I might have realized they were gunning for me and managed a getaway.

But now it was too late.

"Just the person we wanted to talk to." Velda blocked my path, her liver-spotted hand landing on my forearm.

Caught like a fly on sticky paper. The tiny voice in my head screamed at me to run, but good manners kept me rooted in place. *Be respectful of your elders* had been drummed into me since I was a toddler, and they were all Billie's age or close to it. Definitely *elders*. I struggled to be polite, offering a wary, "Oh?"

"We figure you'll have all the details," Jeanette said, her bony hand landing on my left shoulder, the sharp nails biting through my sweatshirt. She wore two insulated cotton tops on her thin frame, covered by an ankle-length jumper. Her hair was in schoolgirl braids. Her gaze resembled that of a wharf cat on the hunt.

I pulled to my right but bumped something solid. Wanda. Her sturdy chef's body blocked my escape. Did none of them understand the concept of personal space? I felt like a shrimp about to be gobbled up by three crabs. I considered my options. As much as I'd like to shake them all off and run for my life, I didn't want to create a scene on Front Street. God knows there'd been enough of that lately.

If they weren't going to be reasonable, I would have to be. I exhaled, striving for a benign expression. "I'm really sorry that I don't have time to stop and chat with you this morning, ladies, but as you know, the expo starts in a couple of hours, and I'm on a tight schedule."

"You're wearing your running clothes," Wanda said, seeing right through my ruse.

"Yes," I said, "running helps my stamina." And today would require every ounce I could muster. "So, if you'll excuse me, time is slipping away."

No one moved. I swallowed a lump of annoyance. I hadn't forgiven any of them for snooping into my mother's love life. Or their grievous treatment of Whitey. If I wasn't careful, my temper would get the better of me, and I didn't want to waste a minute fretting about regrets later in the day. "I need to go."

Velda leaned closer, and my olfactory senses objected. Had she eaten raw onions for breakfast? The soft breeze picked at her flyaway gray hair, and I prayed for a gale-force wind to knock her sideways so that I could escape. "Well, we need the scoop."

I rolled my eyes. Wanting *the scoop* was an ongoing reason to live for these three. And since I wasn't sure what they were after, I said, "I don't have any scoop. Nope. None."

"Hah." Wanda snorted. "You were there."

"An eyewitness," Velda said.

"We heard Seth recorded the whole thing. I'll bet they're going to put it on YouTube, aren't they?" Jeanette sighed as if she might swoon, giving me a glimpse at the younger, dreamier woman she'd likely once been. "I can't wait to see it."

Since Seth packed a camera the way gunslingers in the Old West used to carry pistols, he was always armed and shooting photos or videos. And that meant I hadn't a clue what they were fishing for. "I don't have any scoop about anything."

"Don't pull that innocent look on us." Wanda gave a disgusted grunt. "You know we're talking about the engagement."

I didn't have to ask whose engagement. My stomach dipped. How had these three found out about it already? It only happened last night. On the other hand, this was Weddingville. It was inevitable news would spread like wildfire about something as eventful as two local, longtime sweethearts getting engaged. After all, no one who attended the proposal last night had been sworn to secrecy.

I rubbed a hand across my eyes, wishing I could clear my head of Meg looking caught in the headlights as Troy popped the question. Where was her elation? Her joy? Had she agreed to marry him in response to Peter eloping with Ash? Heck, had she even agreed to marry Troy? I snapped my fingers. *That's it. That's what's bothering me.* Her nonverbal response wasn't actually a yes. And knowing Meg…

"Come on, girl, open up," Jeanette urged.

"About time Meg came to her senses," Velda said.

I could've debated Meg and her senses being in sync, but imagining the battery of questions *that* would cause, I held my tongue. "I really have to go."

Wanda said, "Gwen is so excited she called first thing this

morning to book an appointment for her and Meg to sample reception cakes."

My giveaway face flashed surprise. I mean, seriously, already choosing a cake made it seem like Meg and Troy intended to marry really soon. The thought nearly choked me. Did they? Now I wanted *the scoop*. "Surely Gwen mentioned when the wedding was taking place?"

"She was elusive," Wanda said.

"That's why we came to find you," Velda added.

"If anyone knows the date of the wedding, it's you, Daryl Anne," Jeanette said, tightening her grip. "After all, you're bound to be the maid of honor, right?"

Meg hadn't asked me yet, but I assumed I would be. I nodded, and the nails biting into my shoulder retracted.

Jeanette said, "We expect to be invited to this one. You tell Troy and Meg that for me, okay?"

"Is Meg going to wear the same dress as last time?" Velda asked. "Or something totally different?"

The thought of Meg's other wedding gown made me cringe. That dress held so many bad memories and vile stains, it belonged on a pyre. "How could you even ask that?"

Velda blanched. "Oh dear. I suppose that was in poor taste. Sorry."

"Well, personally," Wanda said, gazing down her nose in disapproval, "I think it's too soon."

"T-too soon?" Velda sputtered. She let go of me and plastered her hand on her sagging bosom. "It's not like Meg's other groom died. She dumped his cheatin' ass."

"Well, there is that," Wanda admitted. "Still…"

"It's not too soon," Velda said a little louder. "It's years late is what it is."

"I always knew they'd end up together." Jeanette's face went dreamy again, and she released me to shake a finger at the baker. "Those two are soul mates. I did their charts."

The three women shifted toward each other, and I found myself outside their little group. Before they could notice, I took off at a clip. Almost immediately, I heard footfalls behind me. I didn't look around. If I couldn't outdistance three senior citizens, then I would donate my new running shoes to the church bazaar.

"Hey, Blessing, slow down a second," Seth called out. In my peripheral vision, I saw he was gaining on me. I decelerated, letting him catch up. Tension eased from my body, replaced with relief and gratitude. Like a knight in shining armor, Seth seemed to always show up when needed. I slid to a halt and spun around to thank him.

He slammed into me, nearly knocking us both to the ground. But he wasn't alone. Sonny, his big, yellow Lab, skidded to a stop, giving an excited yelp, as if we were playing a new game. He darted around us. Twice. His leash lashed us together as effectively as thread to a spool.

Sensation carried me away. I lost all awareness of where we were, of the traffic on the street, of shoppers and locals strolling past us on the sidewalk. I was only aware of Seth and the feel of him. I hadn't expected to find myself pressed full length to the sexiest man in town, but the sensation was like that first sip of morning coffee, warm, bracing, and delicious. That one thing that started your day with a smile. I peered up into his laughing eyes.

"Nice running into you, Blessing."

"You too, Quinlan."

From up the street, I heard Velda say, "Well, would you look at that? Folks in this town are getting more action than the local casino."

I grimaced, smothering a groan in the comfort of Seth's solid chest. I wasn't sure when, but sometime later today, Mom or Billie were likely to get a visit from the Gossip Sisters wanting the scoop on *my* love life.

Sonny whined, done with the game. He tugged on the leash as though we'd tangled him instead of the other way around. Seth and I laughed, but the dog was not amused. Seth managed to free his hands, and as he consoled the dog, he freed us from the leash. I stepped back, disappointed at the sudden loss of Seth's heat, yet feeling a bit awkward at the public display, unsure how to deal with the need I couldn't tamp or tap. I bent to give the mutt a hug and suffered a slobbery kiss that pulled a laugh from me.

A shop bell tinkled, bringing me back to our surroundings. Seth offered me a clean hankie to wipe off the dog drool as I stood. We were outside of the Ring Bearer, the local jeweler. Sonny barked excitedly as he saw who was emerging.

Troy and Meg had been chatting quietly, but the dog's greeting brought their heads up.

"Hey, good morning," Troy said, giving Sonny's head a pat.

Seth said, "I think we can guess what you were doing in there."

Troy grinned, looking like the happiest man on Earth. Meg smiled, too, but it was more a nervous parting of her lips, like she'd been caught doing something secret and now the whole town would know. I could have told her the whole of Weddingville already did know, but I doubted she wanted to hear that.

"Did you decide to go with a more traditional ring after all?" I asked, directing my question to Meg, figuring she'd realize I was asking about more than the ring.

"It's a beautiful ring," Meg said.

It really was. The ruby was huge, offset by a surround of small diamonds.

"And it's one of a kind. Like my love," Troy said, squeezing Meg's arm. "But some of the tips holding the stones in the setting need to be rebuilt."

"And the fit is wrong." Meg met my gaze, and I wondered if she was being subtle about her fit with Troy. It seemed as though she were silently pleading with me to get her out of this situation. Since I'd felt similarly trapped by the Gossip Sisters a few minutes earlier, I really wanted to help her. I just wasn't sure which situation she wanted out of. The proposal and impending wedding or this awkward moment with the guys.

I could choose just one and decided, at the moment, only the latter was in my control. "Did you forget about our breakfast date, Meg? We have some planning to do without any males."

"I was just going to text you," she said, brightening.

She didn't mention that I was in my running clothes or even seem to register that she'd forgotten our jog, but I didn't want to have a heart-to-heart as we traversed our favorite trails. I wanted a sit-down, face-to-face discussion. "I've just got time to grab a bite and then I have to get back to the shop. Another day of expo craziness starts in an hour and a half."

Troy's phone buzzed. He checked it. "That's the sheriff. If I don't get to the station immediately, my butt will be hamburger." He planted a kiss on Meg's forehead.

Sonny barked, and Seth grinned. "And I have to finish this guy's walk or I'll never hear the end of it." He looked like he wanted to kiss me on the forehead, too, or elsewhere, and I wanted him to more than I wanted to breathe. He chose instead to wink at me. "See you later, Blessing."

Before he left, he lifted his camera and took a picture of me and Meg, catching us gazing at each other with solemn expressions charged with private meaning. "You two are really beautiful, you know that?"

I rolled my eyes, but he was serious, and that sobered me. He didn't look at the world through everyday eyes but with his own special vision. He found beauty in emotion, in the mundane, in what others might call plain or average. And he captured that beauty in his photographs. I knew. He'd shown me a portfolio of images he'd taken over the years. I was encouraging him to put them together into a book.

I discussed this with Meg on the way to Cold Feet Café, keeping the conversation light, the topics anything and everything except what we both wanted to talk about until we'd ordered and had coffee in front of us. I opened with, "So, you're going to marry Troy? For real?"

Meg's lips pressed together, forming a thin line, and she was silent a long moment. "I feel numb. Like the last day and a half happened to someone else, not to me. Does that even make sense? It was like I was Seth, watching it all through the lens of a camera. Like it was happening to another Meg. Not this Meg. Not me."

Yep, Meg and her senses were as far apart as ever. If anyone else said this to me, I might think they were having a nervous breakdown. But this was Meg. She wore her heart on her sleeve. Eight weeks earlier, someone had cut it off and stomped on it, but before she'd come to terms with that pain, another someone had picked her heart up and held it to his own heart, cherishing it. Naturally she wanted to grasp hold of the one professing undying love. Who wouldn't? But was that the real thing or gratitude?

I said, "That doesn't sound like you're ready for this. Is it that you aren't sure that you can trust Troy yet?"

Her eyes widened. I'd touched a nerve. "How did you know that?"

"Uh, I'm your best friend. And you told me just a couple of days ago."

"Oh, yeah. I forgot."

The waitress brought our food. I was surprised at how hungry I was. Meg seemed to have found her appetite, too, and I realized she probably felt less alone and lost now that she knew someone else understood the doubts plaguing her.

"So, do you want to marry Troy?" I kept my voice down.

Meg chewed her pancakes, her brow knit as if she were really thinking about it. "I've wanted to marry him for as long as I can remember, until I didn't. Until he took off and joined the navy and told me in a text."

"But..." Of course there was a but.

"I do still love him, Daryl Anne. I didn't know how much until I saw him again. I guess I just never got over him."

This didn't surprise me at all. She'd been in love with Troy since they were both five. I reached over and touched her hand. "It's okay."

"No, it's not. I almost married Peter. I would've been his wife if we hadn't decided to have the ceremony in this town." She shook her head, her red curls bouncing. "I dodged a bullet, didn't I?"

Hoping she wouldn't be offended, I decided to be honest. I nodded. "Definitely."

She ate more pancake. I finished a slice of toast, then asked, "Do you still have feelings for Peter?"

She set down her fork and dabbed the corners of her mouth with a napkin. "I admit I was pretty confused for a while there.

I did love him, but a couple of weeks ago, I realized that I was getting over him way too quickly if he were the love of my life. I must not have ever been *in* love with him. Infatuated, probably. And let's face it, the guy I thought he was only existed in my mind. The real Peter is a self-centered egomaniac."

"And Ash…?"

"Knows what she's getting. He won't be faithful. He's incapable of it. But I don't think she cares. Peter is a stepping stone. He'll be hard pressed to get rid of her until she decides to move on. She's ambitious. More than I realized. When she wants something, she goes after it like a rabid dog. I used to admire that trait in her, but now, well, I almost feel sorry for Peter. Almost."

I grinned. *Karma is a bitch, and Peter Wolfe married her.* "So, you and Troy…have you set a date or are you taking it slow and easy?"

"He's in a rush."

"And you?"

"I'm not sure I can face planning another wedding this soon." She stirred cream into her coffee. "I wish we could elope."

I remembered Jeanette Corn saying, *"I expect to be invited to this wedding."* "Good luck with that. The whole of Weddingville has anticipated you marrying Troy since you were in your teens. There would be an uprising if you ran off and tied the knot in secret."

Meg groaned. "I know. Please don't make me go through this without you. Please say you'll be maid of honor?"

"Always," I answered from my heart, ignoring the little nagging voice inside that was screaming, *No, never, ever, no, no, no.* The truth was, if she wanted me, I would stand up for Meg if she married a dozen times. I just would. I drank the last of my coffee and tossed two fives onto the table to cover my share of the meal and tip. "I need to get to the shop."

"Speaking of the bridal shop, isn't that woman at the counter the temp your mom hired?"

I peered out from the booth. Jenny stood next to the cash register paying for something she'd purchased that fit into a pastry box. "Oh, dear. Gram must've sent her for some cinnamon rolls." Big Finn's pastries were ooey-gooey delicious and off-limits with Billie's diabetes, but she couldn't resist indulging every couple of weeks.

I scooted out of the booth, gave Meg a hug, told her we'd talk more later, then hurried toward Jenny, catching her on the sidewalk. "Hey."

"Oh, hi, Daryl Anne. I didn't realize you were in the café."

"Meg and I were in the end booth." I nodded toward the box she carried. "Whatcha got there?"

"Oh, your grandmother sent me for these."

"Coffee and food runs are usually Hannah's concern."

"I guess Hannah had a personal errand. I saw her going into the jewelry shop on my way here."

I nodded. "I take it Billie sent you for cinnamon rolls?"

"Uh, no. Only blueberry-banana muffins today. She said Mr. Reilly told her last night that he was trying some new pastry recipes."

I hadn't heard about this, but all Billie needed was more irresistible, forbidden treats. That darned sweet tooth would be the death of her, but not if I could help it. "I'm guessing my grandmother failed to inform you that she's supposed to limit her sweets and fats."

"First I've heard of it," Jenny said, concern creasing her forehead.

"Yeah, well, she's not that great about watching her diet."

"Oh. I see. But don't worry. These muffins are sugar-free."

Well now, Big Finn was just full of surprises. And so was Billie. I grinned to myself, realizing as we walked that activity on the street was picking up.

The *whoop-whoop* of a police siren sounded behind us. I jumped, spinning around. Troy looked fierce behind the wheel of his official cruiser as he edged toward the curb, lights flashing. I grabbed Jenny and pulled her back.

"What's going on?" she said, eyes wide.

"I don't know." The bad feeling I'd had right after the wedding proposal returned, unsettling my breakfast and flushing a chill through me. "I think the Weddingville police have had more action the past couple of days than they've had since... since..."

The murder.

Chapter 5

I'm no stranger to crazy, having lived and worked in Hollywood for over five years. I knew it would be insane. I thought I was prepared. Armed with experience. But my memories of past wedding expos failed me when it came to the flat-out madness of women shopping through racks of designer wedding gowns at slashed prices. Or to the noise level ramped to earsplitting volumes. By six p.m., the shop looked like it had been tossed by burglars.

The personnel hadn't fared much better. Billie's usually neat chignon tilted to one side with bobby pins popping up like timers on a done turkey. Mom kept yawning, and Jenny's slicked-back ponytail looked more like a pom-pom. Only Hannah seemed unaffected. Then again, she didn't deal with the public.

"Is it going to be like this every day?" Jenny asked as she gathered a tiara and veil from the red love seat to replace on a window mannequin.

"I hope not," I said, stretching my neck and shoulders. My body ached in places I didn't know I had. And I consider myself to be in pretty good shape. "Is this really worth it?"

Mom's brows lifted as if she thought I'd mislaid my brain.

"We sent a lot of dresses out the door today. And that is, after all, the goal."

Feeling the need to defend my question, I said, "I was talking about my last customer. Major bridezilla, who left without finding a dress. She promised to return." I groaned quietly but received zero sympathy. Probably what I deserved. Bridezillas were often the norm in this business.

"I'm anxious to get to the computer and add up the receipts," Billie said. She pulled a tablet from the deep pocket of her slacks. "I also have a few alterations to schedule."

She smiled as she said this, and I felt a bit of the weariness lift from me. As frenetic as the biannual expos could be, they accounted for the largest part of our yearly income. The more wedding gowns, accessories, and alterations we sold, the better our bottom line. If this kept up, it would be our best year ever.

The only caveat was that Gram would no longer be doing the bulk of the alterations. Hannah and I would. Breaking the same wrist twice in a six-week time span had diminished her skill for delicate stitching, and the heart attack that incited the second break also robbed her of her patience for the handwork.

I was so used to Billie always bouncing back quickly from illnesses that when she didn't this time, it really brought me up short. Age was catching up to her. I had to look at how her declining health would affect the future of the bridal shop and how that would affect my mother. *Sometimes it takes a crisis to clear away the clouds and fog, to reveal what our priorities are, where our hearts really long to be.* I had only one choice. And I was okay with it. I gave up my dream job in Hollywood and returned home, content that the move would likely be permanent.

It helped that Meg had also moved back. And Seth living here might've been a factor, too.

"It just goes to show that crime does pay," Gram said, catching us all by surprise.

"What?" I figured she meant the recent robberies. Yep, I said robberies. Plural. Another one had occurred this morning as Meg and I were having breakfast. That's where Troy was headed when Jenny and I returned to the bridal shop with the sugar-free muffins. But Gram was talking about a different crime.

She waved her hand as if the words were written on the air. "The murder, the famous actor angle, all those reporters, they put Weddingville on the map even more than it already was."

She had a point.

"What murder?" Jenny cast a questioning glance from one to the other of us, a mask of bewilderment on her pretty face.

She has no idea what Gram is referring to, I thought, puzzling the oddity of that.

"How could she not have heard about the murder?" Hannah whispered to me.

"I don't know." I gave Hannah a don't-follow-me glance, then left Mom and Gram to explain to Jenny. I headed to the office for some much-needed coffee. Even if Jenny had had no access to TV or radio, even if she'd been living out of the country, she'd surely have heard by now what went on in Weddingville eight weeks ago. One of the key players in the tragedy was a world-renowned movie star, which caused the sensational story to be plastered throughout the world on every known media outlet.

The police investigation revealed a secret betrayal that Meg couldn't forgive and that made Peter the butt of late-night jokes on every network. It even broke Twitter twice. Yet Jenny hadn't heard about it?

As I approached the office, I caught movement in the lunchroom area and smelled the rich aroma of freshly brewed coffee.

Seth. Bless his heart. Always there with a solution to ease whatever he could. On the other hand, his day hadn't been much easier than mine. He probably needed a caffeine jolt as badly as I did. Why did frazzled translate to sexy on him? Why did his rumpled hair and a touch of sleepiness around his eyes send tingles of lust through me? Why did his wrinkled shirt fill me with an urge to run my hands up his chest, over his shoulders, and down his arms? My mouth watered, and I forced myself to stop advancing on him, afraid I'd act on my impulses, more fearful still that someone else would decide to come seeking coffee and find us…interrupt us. But damn, even the camera attached to his belt gave me goose bumps.

Seth didn't look up as I approached. His head was bent over his phone.

"Something important?" I asked.

"Yeah, kind of." He sighed, then glanced at me, and his lips lifted at the edges in a soft, inviting smile, but he didn't elaborate. I didn't push.

He went back to staring at his phone. His photography studio was in his home, three blocks off Front Street and less accessible to foot traffic. He was renting the far end of our salon for the duration of the expo. The thought of working with him every day had seemed like a sweet fantasy, but the reality was that we hadn't had a moment alone until now. And he wasn't paying any attention to me. I tried another tact. "Was it as hectic for you today as it was for us?"

"It was actually." Keeping his phone in his palm, he filled a mug with his free hand and offered it to me, finally meeting my eyes. He seemed like he wanted to say something more but wasn't sure how to say it.

"A penny for your thoughts, Quinlan." I suppressed a grin.

He chuckled. "I guess you're going to find out sooner or later. I know you heard it was the Ring Bearer that was robbed this morning."

I nodded. "I suspect every Weddingville citizen has heard about it by now. It's making a lot of folks nervous. Edgy."

Seth nodded, but something in his eyes made my heart clutch. I clasped my mug as dread splashed through me. Had someone been harmed during the holdup? Shot or…? An unbidden vision of the stolen cake server set flashed into my mind. "What happened? Did the robber have a gun or knife or…something?" *Could you even stab someone with the serrated edge of a cake knife?*

"No, no one was hurt," Seth said.

"Well, thank God for that," Billie said, coming toward us. "I'm glad Susan had Whitey install security cameras here. Anyone rips us off, we'll catch them on tape."

"Yes, we will." I didn't bother telling her it was digital feed these days, not tape, that the cameras recorded, but I was also glad for the security measures. Then again, the jewelry shop had security before anyone else in town, and it hadn't deterred the thief. I kept that thought to myself. No reason to cause Gram worry.

"It's a shame the rest of this town hasn't been more eager to hire Mr. Grobowski," Seth said.

"It is." Gram poked hairpins into her chignon in an effort to secure it. The exercise proved futile. "Since the murder, Weddingville has become a destination site for more than the wedding services we offer. People are coming to sightsee. No telling what kind of element we're attracting. Next thing you know, we'll have gangs and people getting shot down in the street."

I rolled my eyes. "Let's not get carried away, Gram." Where was her usual don't-borrow-trouble attitude?

"You have an in with Troy and the sheriff, Seth." Gram abandoned the effort of fixing her hair without a mirror and reached for her coffee. "Did they tell you what the crook stole from the jewelry shop?"

"No," he said, too quickly. Billie accepted his answer, but I was starting to know him a lot better, and I could tell he was holding back. He knew. He'd probably been called in to film the aftermath shortly after the robbery happened, which would explain his late arrival today.

"I need to clean up my area and see what materials I'll have to replace for tomorrow," Seth said, leaving as Mom, Jenny, and Hannah arrived for a last cup of coffee.

I followed Seth to the salon. "What's going on, Quinlan? You're too distracted."

"Only by you, Blessing." He reached for me, but I stiff-armed him, holding him at bay.

"Sweet talk won't make me forget"—permanently—"what I want to know. Out with it. What was taken from the Ring Bearer?"

Seth looked suddenly more sad than anything else. My stomach dipped. I'd rather have him closed-mouthed than see that regret in his sexy eyes. "What is it?"

"Meg's ring was taken."

I heard a gasp and thought it was my own, but Seth was looking past me. I spun around, half expecting my sneaky cousin to be standing there. But who I saw was worse. Meg.

"Granny O'Malley's ruby ring was stolen?" she sputtered, her eyes the size of giant green marbles. The color drained from her face, her freckles standing out like paint splotches across her pert nose. She opened her mouth to speak. Once. Twice. Three times. Finally she managed, "Why didn't Troy tell me?"

That's what I was wondering. I shot a meaningful glance at Seth. "Yeah, why didn't he?"

Seth looked as disgruntled as a man stuck carrying someone else's burden. "It's a detail they, the police, are holding back. Only the thief will know what was taken."

Meg's frown deepened, but the confusion faded from her eyes, replaced by a growing horror. I held my breath for an impending emotional storm. She didn't disappoint. "It's a sign. It's that ring. It's cursed, you know. Granny O'Malley told me so when I was fifteen."

"She did?" How come I'd never heard about this? "What curse? You never told me about a curse."

"This wedding is doomed, too, isn't it, Daryl Anne?" Meg sobbed. "And I haven't even looked for a gown yet."

Leave it to my best friend to reduce the disaster of a family heirloom disappearing to a sign from God that she'd never find a happy union. I shook my head. The theft was a sign of something all right. Criminal activity. "There are no such things as old Irish curses."

There aren't, are there?

"But in case there are," I added, totally covering my bases, "it's probably a good thing that you won't actually be wearing *that* ring when you wed Troy."

Meg's drowning green eyes stilled on me. "Are you crazy? I can't marry Troy without *that* ring. It's his family tradition."

Oh. Wow. She'd slipped off the edge of the pier and was sinking into the salty waters of illogic. It couldn't be called a tradition, could it, if Troy's granddad gave it to his bride, and his grandson, not his son, passed it on to his bride? It had skipped a generation. I struggled for something to say that would bring her back to the surface of sanity. It came to me in a flash. If the ring was such a tradition, then why had Troy offered her a ring of her choice if she didn't want to wear the ruby one?

I stopped short of asking this as something else snagged my curiosity. "Exactly what kind of curse did Granny O'Malley tell you was on the ring?"

Seth produced a box of tissues, and Meg snatched a few, blowing her nose and dabbing at her tears.

"Do you remember me telling you that she was a Traveler? Her whole family was." Meg glanced from me to Seth, explaining, "Irish gypsies. They traveled the countryside in caravans, camping and living together."

Seth listened, his brow furrowed.

Meg lowered her voice as if afraid she'd be overheard. "She had 'the vision.' She *knew* things. Like fortune-tellers do."

I restrained from rolling my eyes, but a memory stirred. Granny O'Malley in her long black skirts and puffy-sleeved blouses, always waving her arms when she talked. She wore jangling bracelets on each wrist that clanged like a wind chime made of silverware and gave me the gollywobbles as a kid. You know, that queasy feeling in your stomach when you face something creepy. I shuddered now, recalling. I'd always thought of her as a wicked witch, the kind who'd eat Hansel and Gretel. She spoke in a Gaelic tongue that I never could decipher—which made her that much scarier.

I pinned my best friend with a glare. "What curse, Meg?"

"I'm not sure. I can't remember exactly. I recall feeling sick at the thought. That her warning was dire. Something about the marriage failing within the first couple of months."

What? Who would put that kind of a curse on a wedding ring? It was cursed if you wore it? Or cursed if you didn't wear it? It didn't make sense. "Are you sure you have that right?"

"Positive," Meg wailed. "I can't marry Troy."

"Huh?" Seth blurted, obviously taken aback by this new development. I could tell his mind was scrambling for a way to make this right. He excelled at rescuing damsels in distress.

Meg might be more than he could handle. I caught her hands in mine, cooed soothing words that I hoped were heard over her soft moans, and realized I could use some comfort myself. The wedding planning hadn't even begun, and I was once again failing at my major maid-of-honor duty of keeping the bride calm. But how did I fight a curse? Exorcism? A séance? I had no idea. I was out of my depths. My logical side categorized all things paranormal as fiction—great for books and movies and tales around a campfire, but not believable in real life.

Meg, on the other hand, leaned toward all things being possible. Her belief kept me from being too rigid, more open-minded. I pulled her into a hug, and as she cried on my shoulder, I determined that anyone who believed in possibilities deserved a better outcome. I wished her all the love her heart could handle. If marrying Troy would give her that happiness, then someway or another, that needed to happen.

I had to do something. But what? I looked at the problem from all angles and finally realized there was only one way I could fix this for Meg. My solution? Find the person who was robbing the shops in Weddingville and get back that ruby ring. Heck, I'd helped take down a murderer a couple of months ago. A thief was child's play. Right?

Chapter 6

The next two days, I thought of little else but how to go about finding a thief. My distracted state was not lost on my customers. Or my mother. At the end of the second day, I was no nearer to a plan of action as I busied myself putting the salon area back in order.

I learned some of my sleuthing skills from watching TV reruns of old-time cop shows. It looks so easy when Joe Friday says, "Just the facts, ma'am." Or when Steve McGarrett says, "Book 'em, Danno." In real life, there is no snappy catchphrase that will make criminals putty in my hands. Which sucks, darn it. And even worse, a certain woman can be charged with interfering with an official police investigation if she isn't very careful.

Even if the expo weren't impeding my private, secret investigation of the missing ruby ring, and it was, I had to proceed with caution. But how? I felt like Dorothy on the yellow brick road, standing at a crossroads with four different directions to choose from and no hint of which path to take. Where was a scarecrow when I needed one?

My gaze went to the wall-mounted camera. Mom had been reluctant to invest in a security system when she'd first started dating Whitey. If it hadn't worked out between them, she'd be stuck dealing with him, or his company, for the life of the equipment. I rubbed my neck. While I approved of her caution, I couldn't help but wish that the bridal shop cameras were installed before the cake server set was taken from Something Old, Something New. A prospective suspect or two might've been caught on film. At least then I'd have a place to start. As it was, I could count on one finger the clues I had to work from to solve this crime. I huffed out a breath and eyed the changes I'd made to the mannequin in the showroom window with satisfaction.

"Nice," Seth said, startling me. Lost in my investigative thoughts, I'd forgotten he was still here.

"Thanks. Sometimes a different belt or headpiece will transform a gown. Give it a totally different feel." I glanced in his direction, smiling, catching him lowering his camera. Our eyes met for a second; then he went back to straightening his displays in readiness for tomorrow.

My heart picked up speed as I watched his graceful movements, noting the give and stretch of the fabric on certain areas of his hard body, his broad shoulders, his trim waist, his tight butt. My temperature seemed to rise with every flex of muscle, no matter how slight. I gave myself a shake. If I didn't concentrate on something else, I might attack Seth right here, right now. Maybe some coffee would distract me.

Coffee. Pre-Wedding Jitters. Lisa Marie. *Now there was an idea*. She might be a font of helpful tidbits that I could use. Customers told her things all the time. She was the bartender of baristas. Hadn't she given me the good information about the robbery at Bernice's store, info that she'd gleaned from the temp hired to work at Something Old, Something New? I nodded to myself, but the gesture wasn't lost on the man in the room.

"Penny for your thoughts, Blessing," Seth said, staring at me curiously.

I blinked, catching his gaze. Damn, but those eyes made me feel naked and hot. In the sexiest possible way. I took a step toward him, sure that my face was giving away my intention of attacking him right there in the bridal shop for anyone passing by to see. "I was just thinking I could use"—*a kiss, a hug, a tumble in your bed*—"some coffee. How about you?"

Chicken. Why didn't you tell him what you really crave?

"Is that so? I kind of had the impression that it was me you wanted." He closed the gap between us with panther-like stealth, backing me into a wall, pinning me there, towering over me. I inhaled, catching a scent as fresh as a summer morning with a touch of mint. As he leaned toward my mouth, I also smelled desire.

"If you keep reading my mind, Quinlan, I'll have to break open my piggy bank and pay back all those pen—" The last word was lost as his mouth silenced me, the connection of our lips like a series of mini explosions, one after the other until my thoughts whirled.

He pulled back, his voice a breathless whisper. "I'm not after your money, sweetheart, in case you haven't noticed."

Oh, I'd noticed. But I had no time to tell him before he was kissing me again, my toes curling, my insides as fiery and wet as a river of molten butter. His big hands cupped my bottom, pulling me tight against his hips, making sure I felt his need. My bones seemed to dissolve. The urge to strip him of the clothes that impeded my ability to touch every naked inch of Seth tugged at me, but another, sober part of me was screaming, *Not here. Not here.*

I tried to silence the party-spoiler voice, but I swear it kept getting louder. Sounding something like a *tap-tap-tapping*. I knew that sound. What was it? It stopped, and I forgot everything, except the tingling delight of being in Seth's arms with his lips taking me into the stratosphere. *Tap. Tap. Tap.* Was that my conscience?

I broke off the kiss for a second. Listening. Nothing. "Did you hear that?" I whispered to Seth.

"Only the roar of my pulse in my ears," he muttered, his voice ragged with desire.

I decided that was it and let him take me away again on the Passion Express. *Tap. Tap. Tap.* I startled. "Seth, wait."

I peeked my head around the edge of his broad bicep. We were in the salon, the display windows were uncovered, and the Gossip Girls were peering in like visitors at the snake exhibit of a zoo. Tapping on the glass. Grinning like mischievous monkeys. *If only they would hear no evil, see no evil, and speak no evil.* I groaned. Seth started to turn and look, but I stopped him, explaining.

He burst out laughing, and I covered his mouth, not wanting to bring Mom, Gram, and Jenny running in from the storeroom where they were restocking the racks. "Shh. They're going to tell the whole town we were making out."

"Let them," he laughed again, then sobered. "Wait. Do you care?"

Did I? In the scheme of things, I had to admit, I didn't. Not for myself or even for Seth. "Not about them. Just about embarrassing Mom or Gram."

"Well, you're over twenty-one, right?"

"Right…"

"Far as I know, it's not against the law for two consenting adults to...do what we were doing."

"True..."

He grabbed me, spun toward the window, tipped me backward, and kissed me in full view of the Gossip Girls. My eyes fluttered shut, as delicious shivers spread from my lips and headed south. Muted gasps and giggles faded away on a cloud of passion. Too soon, Seth pulled me upright and then turned toward our audience and bowed, tipping an invisible hat. I was still reeling, and the gossipy trio looked ready to swoon. I couldn't blame them. Every new aspect of himself that Seth revealed endeared him to me all the more.

"You're amazing," I said when our nemeses had departed to spread the news.

"And you haven't even seen all of my tricks yet."

"Oh, yeah? Like what?"

"Like this." He pulled me to him, tight, his grip firm and exciting, and then he was kissing me again. Only this time, I thought he might never stop, and I didn't want him to. I opened my lips to welcome his exploring tongue, heard him groan against my mouth, and felt myself slipping into a wonderful fantasy come true. That's when the ornery little voice in my head reminded me that we were still in the salon, still in view of anyone and everyone passing by. Or sneaking up on us. Like Hannah. I cringed. Pulling back from Seth, I saw that his eyes were glazed with passion. Regret filled me. But I didn't give in to it. The first time Seth and I made love was not going to be for public consumption.

As he reached for me again, I resisted, pushing his arms away. I couldn't catch my breath, but I had to make him listen. "Whoa... sailor...we're moving too fast."

"You don't like fast?" Seth said. The huskiness in his voice stroked my senses, tugged at my resistance. "No worry. I can be slow."

He leaned toward me again. I shook my head. "No. Not here. The cameras."

It took a second for my message to sink in, but his brain must have been dulled with lust because he didn't seem to realize I was talking about the security feed. "Worried those nosy Nancys will show up again—with cameras?"

"Oh, Lord." It was bad enough imagining Gram and Mom, or Whitey, viewing the footage of us necking in the salon. But I hadn't even considered one or more of the Gossip Girls whipping out a cell phone to record our PDA. "Do you really think they photographed us kissing?"

Seth shrugged, grinning that crooked, naughty smile that started my blood heating with new fervor. "It's your own fault, Blessing. I can't think straight around you."

I'd waited so long to hear something like this from Seth that I thought my heart would burst from the wonder of it. I reached to touch his cheek, on the brink of losing myself again in the hunger I read in his eyes, a craving that echoed the one deep inside me. Then another thought slammed into me. "What if they did take photos and they post them on Instagram or Pinterest?"

"You think they have Pinterest pages?"

I didn't know, but probably they did. At least one of them. "Maybe."

Seth burst out laughing again.

"What's so funny?" Mom said as Seth moved away from me, trying to rein in his glee. My cheeks felt on fire. It was one thing for my mother to view footage of Seth and me making out and quite another to have her nearly walk in on us. Granted, she hadn't. But surely she sensed the electricity bouncing between us.

It took me a second to realize, however, that she hadn't even blinked. Huh? Who was this new woman? I had to give Whitey props. He seemed to be a positive influence on her, easing her out of her comfort zone, helping her find the fun-loving woman she'd been before Dad died.

Mom said, "Are either of you going to tell me the joke?"

"It's nothing," I lied. She'd find out soon enough if the Gossip Girls did as predicted, but I wasn't about to fill her in. I wasn't ready to share with anyone. My feelings were too fragile and personal. Too special. I wanted—no, needed—to hold it in my heart a while longer. "Seth was just being silly."

He threw me a bemused grin. The twinkle in his eye suggested he was more than willing to confess everything to my mother. I threw him a don't-you-dare glare, and darn him, he chuckled.

Mom arched a brow. She knew we were being elusive, but she gave up on finding out about what and switched the subject. "I want to ask you a favor, Daryl Anne."

"Okay," I said, still trying to regain my composure and corral the wanton passion Seth had unleashed. My lips felt swollen and abandoned. My hand found its way to the back of my neck, smoothing the wispy ends of my hair, a nervous gesture that I had no control over and that Mom would surely recognize for what it was.

She noticed but didn't comment on it. "As we were sorting and restocking the racks, Jenny mentioned how lovely some of the gowns are. I asked if she had her dress yet. She said that her fiancé's mother has offered her own wedding dress."

"Is Jenny excited about that?" I asked as Seth wandered back to his end of the salon. Mom gestured me to the love seat. It felt great to get off my feet.

"Not exactly."

I wasn't surprised. Often women come to believe over the years that the gown that was perfect for them when they married will be exactly right for the next generation's family bride. But styles change drastically in twenty years. The dress in question is more likely nothing near what the new bride envisions herself wearing on her special day. "Did she turn down the offer?"

Mom glanced toward the storeroom as if to assure herself that Jenny wasn't within earshot. "She says she was touched when Brad's mother made the offer."

"But...?" I asked.

"Then she saw the dress." Mom grimaced. "She showed it to me on her phone. It hasn't aged well. The lace is yellowed, and the style is something straight from the seventies. Think flower child. High neck, huge sleeves, swishy skirt that was beautiful in its day, but..."

"Brides today don't want something as covered up as that. What about redesigning it?" I hadn't tried my hand at that, but I was willing to give it a shot with Billie's guidance.

"She's afraid to even mention that to Brad's mom. Apparently the woman is very attached to this dress."

What a position to be in. Jenny didn't want to say yes and couldn't say no. "What's she going to do?"

Mom sighed. "I have a plan. I'm willing to do a special deal for Jenny on a sale item so that she can have a gown she does see herself wearing at her wedding."

I gave my mother a hug. "She doesn't know how lucky she is to have you in her life."

Mom smiled at my loving embrace and the compliment. "Well, that's not my only plan."

"Oh?" I pulled back, cocking my head to the side.

"She hasn't done much of anything toward planning. I suggested she hire Zelda Love to help with the various tasks required, but she confessed Brad's parents are paying for the wedding, and the budget is very, very limited. She can't afford to hire anyone. So I thought maybe you could guide her, like you did for Meg."

"Me?" Was she talking about my previous stint as maid of honor? "But Meg had Zelda, and I only did the things that—"

"It's going to be a small affair. Nothing much to do. And you're always so organized, dear. You're the perfect one."

"What exactly do you see me doing, Mother?"

"Well, you know, you could take her around to the shops this week. Everyone is running sales."

Including us. Had she lost her mind? During a week that was less slammed than this one, I would gladly help a bride-to-be navigate the daunting job of planning her own wedding. My organized mind thrived on this kind of task. But my agenda for the week ahead was already too tight. How was I supposed to fit this in? "I don't see how—"

"I was thinking you could introduce her to the shop owners or some of their staff at the different shops," Mom interjected before I could finish my refusal. Though how she could think this was sweetening the pot was beyond me. She didn't give me a chance to object. "Make sure she gets my discount on anything she might decide to purchase."

I counted to ten. Slowly. Introduce her to staff? I risked a glance at Seth. The coward was backing away, not about to get between two determined Blessing women. "Mom, I'm already scheduled to meet with Zelda and Meg tomorrow to start planning Meg and Troy's wedding."

Of course, that wedding might not happen, if the ring wasn't found.

"Perfect," Mom declared. "Jenny can tag along and take notes."

How was I supposed to juggle Zelda and Meg and Jenny? And do any sleuthing?

I froze. *Wasn't I just wondering how to get the staff at the Ring Bearer and Something Old, Something New to open up to me about the robberies?* Until now, I'd had no idea how to accomplish that. I bit down on a sudden surge of excitement. Hah. Leave it to Mom to deliver the means I'd been seeking. This was brilliant. I could hunt clues to my heart's content without Troy or Seth accusing me of nosing in on an official police investigation. "Okay. I'll do what I can."

"Oh, good. I knew I could count on you, Daryl Anne." She hugged me, then stood and said, "Whitey is bringing Chinese takeout for Billie and me. He's getting plenty if you two don't have other dinner plans."

The only plans I knew we had were X-rated and did not involve food. Unless we got creative. The thought flushed heat through me. But as disappointment moved across Seth's face like a gray cloud, my inner warmth chilled. He sighed, regretful. "Can I get a rain check, Susan? I've got film to put together for WPD and they need it before morning."

"Of course. Anytime, Seth. You're always welcome." She left us alone.

"Will you also give me a rain check, Blessing?" He didn't need to say for what. The smoldering in his eyes left no room for doubt but doubled my own disappointment.

"I'm holding you to it."

His sexy grin appeared, and longing raced through me as he planted a chaste kiss on my lips. I warned him, "If you start that again, I guarantee you'll be using that rain check here and now."

"Don't tempt me, woman." But I could see that I had tempted him, and my disappointment flew away like a bird heading south for the winter. He grazed his hand down my cheek. "God, I want to stay more than I can say, Blessing, but I'm leaving. When we finally do get together, it won't be rushed. I intend to take my time and for you to enjoy every second of it."

Chapter 7

*C*rayola-blond hair, hot-pink dress, and bubbling enthusiasm. Zelda Love was like a party favor. Sweet. Colorful. Merry. Recently wed to Meg's father, Big Finn Reilly, Zelda retained that honeymoon glow, her happiness spilling over like a chocolate fountain as she welcomed us into her compact shop. "Come in, come in."

We'd arrived armed with giant latte cups of our individual choosing from Pre-Wedding Jitters. Jenny was also toting an electronic tablet, for note taking, I guessed. Meg had a shoe box under one arm, and I had a head full of stress. I'd spent a restless night dreaming of weddings, my own wedding in particular, an old dream that I hadn't had since moving to Los Angeles but one that had occurred pretty regularly throughout my teens. Starting when I'd first fallen for Seth in my impressionable, romantic youth. It seemed a few hot, sexy kisses shared with that man were all it took to rouse long-forgotten fantasies.

"Sit anywhere," Zelda said, directing us around a silk screen that divided what had once served as the living and dining rooms of this converted, century-old, shotgun-style home. She lifted a catalogue from the round table that was positioned directly beneath an antique crystal chandelier. Next to her steaming mug of coffee, she set a ringed binder with *Meg and Troy* lettered on the cover, then sat, her back to the only window.

"Call me old school if you want for using a pen and paper to keep my notes," Zelda said, "but one computer crash that wiped out every speck of information I'd gathered on three weddings taught me a lesson. Always keep a hardcopy."

I flashed back to the binder she'd had for Meg's wedding to Peter. In the last couple of days before the ceremony, it had resembled a sandwich with its stuffing trying to escape. Every contingency planned for...except the one that no one had foreseen. Murder. *Proof that no plan is foolproof.*

"Where do we start?" Jenny asked, breaking into my dark thoughts.

"I like to start with a theme," Zelda said, plunging ahead. "What kind of wedding does the happy couple want? Indoor or outdoor? Formal church, informal garden, beach, barn, or backyard? Is it a holiday wedding? If so, which one? Christmas, New Year's, Valentine's Day, Fourth of July, Halloween? Even St. Patrick's Day. Once I know the theme, then we can move on to selecting the appropriate gown, flowers, food, invitations, et cetera."

Jenny's fingers flew across the virtual keyboard on her electronic tablet as Zelda spoke.

"Meg, honey," Zelda said, "have you and Troy discussed any of that yet?"

Meg sat as stiff as one of the mannequins in the bridal shop window, her face unreadable. And I'm usually pretty good at reading her. Not today. Sure, the redness remaining in her big green eyes bespoke of a night spent crying, but Meg was a wizard

with hair and makeup. Any other signs of distress had been pow-
dered, fluffed, and glossed away.

Her silence concerned me. "Meg?"

"We don't have a theme. Or a date." Meg's sigh sounded like
a resigned moan. She shoved the shoe box into the middle of the
table and flipped off the lid. "But I want the wedding to work
with these."

We all leaned forward, peering into the box as Meg gingerly
edged aside a layer of creamy tissue paper. Nestled inside were
five-inch, bloodred, satin high heels with flat bows across the
toes. A collective "aah" echoed through the room. I felt an odd
little jolt. *I should've recognized that box.* I'd been with Meg the
day she bought these shoes. It was shortly after we'd moved to
Los Angeles, where we'd discovered everything cost more than
we'd planned on. Money was so tight that we'd taken to shopping at a certain vintage clothing store. More of a thrift shop, in
my opinion.

Meg had noticed the heels right off, remarking how brand-
new they appeared to be. The sales clerk recognized an easy
mark when she heard one. She scooted to our sides, regaling us
in the tale of the crimson slippers. She claimed the heels were
worn only once by a young starlet attending her first Oscars
award night. The starlet had won Best Actress that year. The
next morning, she awoke to find the world at her feet, her agent's
phone ringing off the hook, and incredible roles being offered.
Every actor's dream come true. But within the month, the starlet
gave up her career and ran off with her Prince Charming. A real
prince.

I'd watched Meg swallowing the story like a hungry salmon
taking bait. Hook, line, and sinker. Coming off the breakup with
Troy, Meg was in a vulnerable place. She was touched by the story

and by the possibility that her own prince would one day sweep her off her feet and carry her away. I'd tried talking her out of the purchase, pleading for the sake of our budget. She went ahead and tried on the shoes anyway. They fit her like gloves, of course. Meg danced in a circle, laughing, declaring that those satin heels were meant for her. I'd thought her impulsive. Insane. Infuriating. Especially since she'd never worn them. But as I stared at those crimson slippers now, something strange and wonderful reduced my cynical side to a small black lump.

"Can you do that?" Meg asked Zelda. "Build a wedding plan around these heels?"

"Absolutely," Zelda enthused, balancing one shoe on her palm as if it were a precious stone. "There's something magical about these, isn't there? Wherever did you find them?"

Meg told the story as I watched the light in her eyes dancing. She seemed much happier today than yesterday. Was she putting on a show for her new stepmother and Jenny? Or did this mean she'd decided to ignore the curse and accept that Troy was the Prince Charming she longed for?

"Indoors or outdoors?" Zelda asked.

"Definitely indoors. In a church," Meg said. "I don't want a repeat of anything we'd planned for the other—"

"No. Of course not," Zelda interrupted, touching her stepdaughter's hand lovingly. "This is going to be a very happy wedding. And a joyous union." The tissue paper crackled as she gently placed the high heel into the box beside its mate, then took up a pen and jotted notes into her ringed notebook. "And I expect everyone in town will want to be there, so the big church."

"Sure," Meg said, sounding like she meant "whatever."

"I'm having an outdoor wedding," Jenny said softly, as if to herself, but there was envy in her eyes as they steadied on Meg. "In Brad's parents' backyard."

I frowned. While that might seem an ideal setting in which to wed for many people, I guessed from her tone that Jenny had had something else in mind. Like her own church wedding. I hadn't met her future in-laws, but I was getting a less-than-favorable impression of them. I felt sorry for Jenny. She seemed easily persuaded, unable to stand up to anyone stronger willed than herself. A sure target for bullies.

"Do you have a theme?" Zelda asked Jenny.

"Cheap," Jenny said. "We're doing most everything ourselves. Fixing the food. Flowers from the garden."

A dress she didn't want to wear.

"DIY weddings can be lovely, dear," Zelda said, smiling sweetly, offering Jenny hope. "It's who you're marrying, not how you get married, that counts."

"How could you say that?" Jenny looked taken aback. "You're a wedding planner. Don't you believe your customers should have the most elaborate wedding they can afford?"

Zelda didn't take offense. Not that Jenny had meant to be rude. She seemed more shocked by the wedding planner's suggestion than anything else. Zelda laughed. "Well, dear, I don't mind a big commission, but it's not about the size of your bank account. I work with brides on every kind of budget. I try to make even the most inexpensive wedding as special as the elaborate ones."

"So, Meg," I jumped in, purposefully changing the subject, "what kind of dress are you thinking to wear with these incredible heels?"

"Definitely not a ball gown." The gown she'd chosen for her marriage to Peter had been a peachy, full-skirted, Cinderella dress. I would never forget how beautiful she'd looked before the ceremony started or how horrible once it had all gone wrong. She sighed. "Maybe a tea length, and this time I want white. Do you have anything like that on the sales racks?"

Absolutely. And she knew it. She'd helped me organize those racks only a few days ago. I narrowed my eyes. Why had she asked me that? Did she now intend to go ahead with the marriage? Had she given up worrying about the curse? Or was it still messing with her emotions? "Have you set a date yet?"

"I just said we haven't." The hard gaze she returned spoke louder than words. It was what I'd feared. She was going through the motions of planning this wedding, probably for Zelda's sake and likely to keep her father from learning how unhinged she was about the curse. Crap. Troy was probably freaking out, wishing he'd given her a different engagement ring. Because Meg's mind was set. Unless or until Granny O'Malley's ruby ring was found and on her finger, she wasn't getting married. Crimson slippers or no crimson slippers.

* * *

I dragged Meg and Jenny out of Zelda's and down the street to the Ring Bearer. When I say dragged, I mean it was like taking a couple of cats for a walk. If I'd had them on leashes, they'd have pulled my arms in opposite directions, out of their sockets.

Meg balked, scowling. "I really don't want to go into that shop."

"Me neither. I already have an engagement ring," Jenny said, flashing a modest cut diamond set in gold. "And I thought Meg did, too. Isn't your ring getting resized or something?"

Meg and I blanched in unison. We weren't supposed to know what was stolen from the jewelry store. And here we stood, wearing matching guilty expressions. Somehow we had to keep from letting it slip to Jenny that Meg's ring had been swiped. I blurted, "Troy wanted her to look at wedding rings."

"Get us matching ones," Meg said, picking up where I'd left off.

I didn't advocate lying, but sometimes, as a secret sleuth, one had to. I was aware of time slipping away; the air losing its morning chill, the increase in traffic, consumers coming into town, businesses preparing to start another expo day. We'd need to get to the bridal shop very soon. I stopped, hands on hips. I'd hoped to avoid telling them this, but I could see now that it was inevitable. I hadn't thought it out clearly enough. I needed their help. And cooperation. That meant Jenny would need to be told what I was doing, if not why. "Please indulge me. I want you two to distract Mr. Ring so that I can drill the temporary clerk for details of the robbery."

"Why?" Jenny asked, shying away from me.

Meg glared. "She's playing Sherlock again."

Jenny's gaze bounced between me and Meg. "Who's Sherlock?"

"Holmes," Meg said, "the detective."

The leery confusion remained in Jenny's expression. "Are you in a play or something?"

I glanced toward the sky, watching seagulls swoop and dive, and wondered if Jenny had ever read a book or watched anything besides reality TV. "I'm just doing a little private detecting."

"But why? Oh, I know. To help clear Whitey's name." Jenny nodded as if it made perfect sense to her now.

The sudden eagerness that appeared in her eyes worried me. Maybe it was better to cut her loose. "Would you prefer to go back to the bridal shop?"

"No. I wouldn't actually." She was all but rubbing her hands together. "This might be fun."

Another doubt spiraled through me as I imagined all kinds of ways this could go wrong, like someone letting slip that Meg's ring was among the stolen items. Perhaps I should do this alone. No. Elton Ring was as sharp as any diamond facet he'd ever cut. He'd see right through whatever ploy I might come up with and boot me out the door. Meg was key to this but was still looking hesitant.

Maybe I was asking too much of her. It had seemed a simple, unassuming plot. One I'd formed without taking into account my best friend's feelings. I seemed to be doing that a lot to Meg lately. But the truth was, Meg was the best distraction I could hope for. Elton would be eager to help her select another ring. He might even offer to pay for it. After all, hers had gone missing while in his possession. But then he might accidentally mention that and then Jenny would know... "Uh, Meg, maybe we could do this another time."

Like when it was just the two of us.

"No. Let's get it over with," Meg said.

I tilted my head toward Jenny, hoping Meg would take the hint. "Are you sure?"

"Yes." She gave a toss of her fiery curls. The determined set of her jaw told me that she wanted me to find the stolen ring as badly as I wanted to. No matter what laws we bent.

"Well, then, you two know what you need to do...," I said, still tamping down my own misgivings.

"Keep Elton so busy that he doesn't pay any attention to what you're up to," Meg said. "I think we can do that. Right, Jenny?"

"Sure." Jenny removed her own engagement ring, put it in her pocket, and started down the sidewalk. "Let's do it."

But when we arrived at the jewelry shop door, we discovered changes were under way.

A new sign hung in the window: APPOINTMENT ONLY. Obviously no more walk-ins. The necessity for this new reality flushed me with sadness.

"Hey, isn't that Whitey's van?" Meg said, nudging me.

I glanced toward the street and spied the vehicle at the curb. "It is," I said. "Wonder what he's doing here?"

Jenny gave a bark of disapproval. "Can anyone say, 'Closing the barn door after the cows escaped'?"

"They already have a security system." The bitterness in Meg's voice was as thick as a felled tree. Thankfully, Jenny didn't seem to notice. Meg went on. "Fat lot of good it did. Probably installed when the loggers ran this town."

Whitey came around the corner of the building, whistling. A baseball cap covered his pale blond hair, and a tool belt bunched the middle of his coveralls. He had a surveillance camera in hand.

"Hey, good morning," I said. "Whatcha doing here?"

"Hi, Daryl Anne, ladies," he said, nodding to me and then to my companions. "I'm taking Ring's security system out of the Jurassic era. Replacing it with state of the art."

"Told you." Meg nodded. "Too bad you didn't do that sooner."

Whitey shrugged. "Yeah, I tried to get Mr. Ring to consider it last week, but like most everyone else in town, he was reluctant. Never had a robbery, he said. If I was one of those hard-sell guys, maybe he could still say that." As he strode to his van, we trailed after him.

I sighed, feeling sad again. "The good citizens of Weddingville want to think they can trust their friends and neighbors not to rip them off."

"Maybe they need to get out of this town and take a look at the real world," Jenny said.

Meg huffed. "Hah. Live in Hollywood for a while and you'll lock up your cat."

Whitey opened the tailgate on his van and reached inside for something. "Billie told Susan and me last night that she's going to suggest a town meeting to discuss the increasing stranger danger with the council. She said everyone is enjoying the profits of the town's newfound fame but is unprepared for the increased criminal element that can come with it."

Jenny shuddered, clutching her iPad to her chest as though fearing it would be snatched from her. She wrinkled her nose in disgust. "What's the council going to do, pass a law that requires everyone to install a security system?"

"That works for me." Whitey grinned.

"Would such a law even be enforceable?" Meg didn't seem to pick up on the sarcasm in Jenny's voice.

"Probably, but it would be ludicrous and overkill," I said. "The current crunch of consumers isn't a year-round problem. Just during the expos."

"I don't know about any of that. I'm just telling you what Billie intends to do." Whitey pulled a ladder from the depths of the van and carried it to the front edge of the jewelry store as we trailed after him. "I'm just happy to have the business. I had a couple more folks phone for appointments since this latest robbery."

"Crime is paying off for you, then," Jenny suggested, sounding as if she suspected him of doing something illegal.

Whitey spun toward her, his face growing red, his carefree manner gone. "I don't advocate crime. I'm all about preventing it."

Instead of his protest calming or reassuring me, it caused a wayward thought to stumble through my brain. Could Whitey

be pulling a few heists to stir up business for his company? A hot
ball of guilt boiled inside me for even considering the possibility. But I couldn't remove Whitey from my meager suspect list.
*Okay, so his is the only name on that list at the moment. There will
be others. Once I start doing interviews and collecting actual facts
about the robberies.*

Not that I was going to do any interviews if we couldn't get
into the jewelry store right away. I pulled out my phone and
dialed the number. Elton Ring answered. I identified myself
and told him Meg wanted to see some rings. He immediately
unlocked the door, as I'd suspected he might, and we scrambled
inside.

It was like stepping into an ice cave. It wasn't physically cold
but visually chill. The bluish-white floor tiles, the snowy concrete walls, and the bleached cabinets looking like ice sculptures
covered with glass. Pale blue velvet stools edged a display case of
rings at one end of the room. Subdued New Age music floated
from hidden speakers.

There was no other place quite like this in town. And no one
else quite like Elton Ring, the proprietor. If I were to cast him
in a movie, it would be as the diamond-mine worker rather than
the gem merchant. Surrounded by riches, Elton appeared a poor
man, his shirt fabric of the cheapest quality, his pants sale-rack
rejects. Instead of a tie, he wore a jeweler's loupe on a solid gold
chain around his neck. His attention zeroed in on Meg. I prayed
he wouldn't mention the theft of her ruby engagement ring as I
sought out the clerk, standing at the opposite side of the room,
near the hallway to the inner offices where Elton cut and set
stones.

"Just the person I wanted to see," I said, easing up to the counter beside the nervous-looking clerk, a mousy, college-aged female

with Elton's big nose and bright eyes. His daughter Veronica. Movement in the corner of my eye brought me spinning toward the entrance to the back area. A WPD policeman filled the doorway. Troy. Uh-oh.

"Well now. This is interesting. What brings you all to the jewelry store this morning?" Troy skipped his gaze over the room, then pinned me specifically, as if I wore a T-shirt with flashing neon letters that proclaimed, *I'm interfering with an official police investigation.*

Chapter 8

I had visions of being handcuffed and hauled to Weddingville's police station, dumped into an interrogation room, and grilled like a cheeseburger at Big Finn Reilly's Cold Feet Café. If I were a fictional private investigator, Agatha Christie would delete me from the pages of my own novel. I wouldn't blame her either. Just as I couldn't blame Troy. I knew the consequences of getting caught interfering with a police case. *It's not as though this were my first time. Nope. I'm officially a two-time offender.*

Troy didn't take me to the WPD but to a room at the end of the hall. A shelf with various boxes occupied one wall, and a worktable, positioned within easy reach, was decked out with tools I couldn't name but assumed were a jeweler's tricks of the trade. Troy shut the door behind us. The charged silence pounded against my ears. I retreated to the back wall, weighed down by guilt for dragging Meg and Jenny into this, for making them accessories. Apparently I wasn't that contrite or prepared to face the music, however, since I kept wishing the wall would open up so that I could run outside. But the concrete was unyielding.

My gaze steadied on Troy. Tall, dark, and handsome to a fault.

He was so good-looking, in fact, that I was pretty sure a lot of women didn't appreciate that he could also be a hard-ass. That tilted smile, those dimples, and his disarming tone of voice gave the impression that you could talk your way out of whatever infraction of the law you might be accused of. I knew better. Troy was as serious about being an honest cop as I was about helping a bride find the right dress.

My ass was grass.

My nose twitched at the scent of something chemical that I didn't recognize, but the smell of my fear was too familiar. "It's your granny's fault," I declared before he could get a word out. "Her and that Irish Travelers' curse."

Troy blinked, his blue eyes like the flashers on a squad car. "Daryl Anne, I thought you'd learned your lesson about interfering with an official police investigation."

He pulled that cop trick, clamming up, giving me the fish-eye, letting time pass to unnerve his suspect. Me. It was working. I wanted to spill my guts. But the truth was, I didn't have any guts to spill. I'd just started my investigation. I had nothing but a super-short suspect list. And if I declared that I suspected Whitey, Mom would never forgive me. Before I gave in to the urge to confess all, Troy spoke.

"Wait. What? What do you mean about my granny and an Irish Travelers' curse?" Troy had evidently been so intent on dressing me down that he hadn't, at first, registered my outburst. I had his full attention now. My mouth dried. I stared at his badge, certain I could see my sickly face reflected there. He lifted his hat, his blue-black hair thick and unkempt. He scratched his head, and I had a lightbulb moment. His obvious confusion meant Meg hadn't told him that she wouldn't marry him without his granny's ring. Damn and double damn.

I ran my tongue over my dry lips, wishing to find a zipper there so I could shut it. Seth apparently hadn't informed Troy either that he'd spilled the beans about Meg's ring. Despite how shocked he'd been at her meltdown. Why not? Was this some kind of guy code? He'd only tell Troy if Troy brought up the subject. Seth would probably figure it wasn't his place. I, on the other hand, seemed to have no such scruples since I'd stripped the lid off that can of worms as if I were opening a tin of party peanuts. I groaned. Why did I always get stuck breaking bad news? It wasn't like I wanted to inflict pain on others.

"Daryl Anne, I'm losing my patience." He had his hand on the holstered gun at his hip. Definite incentive for a perp to cooperate. Not that I was a perp. He growled, "Start talking."

I wrung my hands. "Well, er, you know the curse that's on Granny O'Malley's ruby ring—"

"What the hell?" His voice rose a couple of octaves, and his lifted brows declared me certifiable. "What curse?"

Oh, brother. He didn't know about the curse either? Didn't he and Meg ever talk? Actually, what did I know about the curse except from some disjointed ramblings from Meg? I bit my lower lip, a habit of Meg's, not mine. I wasn't sure what I expected other than a sore lip, but maybe I was trying to conjure my inner Meg, as if that would reveal the actual curse to me.

"What curse, Daryl Anne?" Troy asked, impatience oozing from him like a feral scent.

"Well, er, I don't exactly know for sure." My fingers were at the nape of my neck, stroking the ends of my short hair. "I only heard about it last night, after Meg learned that the ruby ring had been stolen."

"What! Meg knows about the ring? How?"

At that moment, I knew how a mouse felt cornered by a cat,

its huge teeth and claws bared. I just didn't have a hole that I could run to and hide. "Th-that was an accident."

"An accident…?"

His face was getting awfully red. He wouldn't keel over and die from spiking blood pressure, would he? Nah. He was too young. Too healthy. But Seth might. I cringed. When he found out I'd ratted him out to Troy. Darn it. I didn't want to get Seth into trouble. He might lose his part-time work for the WPD. Maybe I could come up with some other way to explain how Meg could've learned about the ring being stolen. I blanked. Truth was, only the truth would do. *Just the facts, ma'am.*

Please forgive me, Seth. And Meg. I inhaled to steady my nerves. "There's just no easy way to say this. Meg might not be ready to be engaged."

Troy blinked as though he hadn't heard me right, and then he looked as if I'd punched him in the gut. I swallowed hard. He leaned toward me, the burning in his face so fiery I thought I might burst into flames. "If you've done something to screw things up between Meg and me, Daryl Anne…"

Indignation steeled my spine. "Me? I'm not the one trying to rush Meg into getting married when she hasn't totally dealt with what happened over two and a half months ago."

He reared back as if I'd doused him in ice water. He recovered quickly, doing that cop-stare thing again, only this time I didn't feel a smidgen of pressure to speak. I'd already said too much. Already crossed a line from which there was no retreat. I felt like the Grinch who'd just swiped Christmas, my mean heart shriveling in my chest. "I'm sorry, Troy. I don't mean to hurt you, but I think it's all been too quick for her."

His Adam's apple bobbed. "Then why didn't Meg tell me that?"

"What was she going to say with your folks and my folks and her folks and the big surprise?"

He seemed dazed. "But everyone was so happy…"

I nodded. It was the kindest thing I could do. After all, Troy wasn't just a cop; he was also a friend, even if our relationship was sometimes more that of contentious siblings. "Because it's what they've all wanted for you guys since you were in high school."

"But Meg said yes."

Did she? I still wasn't sure about that. "As hard as this is for you to process, that's how difficult—times twenty—it is for Meg to come to terms with her mother being murdered and with discovering she couldn't trust her fiancé."

"But she can trust me," Troy said.

I had too long a memory to let that statement go unchallenged. "Can she?"

He scowled. "What does that mean?"

"Did you forget you ran out on her and joined the navy without saying good-bye in person?"

He paled. "That was years ago. We were too young to settle down then." He lifted his hat again, finger-combing his hair. "But, yeah. Okay. I could've handled it better. Biggest mistake of my life."

"You can say that again."

"Cut me some slack, Daryl Anne. I know I fucked up. Hurt her. That's why I didn't come to L.A. to see her when I got out of the navy. She deserved better. Deserved me to be better. But I swear to God that I never got over Meg."

But Meg thought she was over you. I didn't say that to him. I wanted him to understand, but I didn't want to be cruel. Besides, I knew now that Meg had never truly gotten over Troy. But if and when she decided to commit to him, well, that was up to her.

Not me. "I'm only saying she might be feeling pressured. Look, you two need to talk without anyone else around. Give her a chance to tell you how she feels. Tamp down your own excitement and just listen to her."

I wasn't sure he could manage that, but it was the best advice I had to give—that is, if Meg would open up to him. And really, shouldn't she, if she wanted to have a true relationship with this guy?

He stood there absorbing what I'd said. Not an easy task for a man with his pride and ego, holding on to his dignity in the face of being told the love of his life might be having misgivings about marrying him. I was a dasher of hopes. A tear slipped down my cheek.

Troy must have seen it. "God, Daryl Anne, are you saying that Meg doesn't love me?"

I shook my head fiercely. "No, I—"

"Troy." Meg banged on the outer door. "What are you doing to Daryl Anne?"

Troy opened the door. Meg stood, hands on hips, bristling. "We weren't doing anything wrong—"

She didn't get the rest of the sentence out. Troy caught her wrist and yanked her into the room. If he thought that would calm her down, he was sorely mistaken. She kicked him in the shin.

"Ow." Troy hopped on one foot. "What the hell?"

I gasped, my gaze flying wide. Oh my God, attacking a police officer, interfering in an official police investigation, the crimes against us were stacking up.

But that was the farthest thing from Meg's mind. "Don't think you can manhandle me, Troy O'Malley. Not now. Not ever. I won't put up with police brutality or with any man who gets physically or verbally abusive."

He stepped back, hands raised in surrender. "You're right. It won't happen again. Ever. I'm sorry, sweetheart. And I'm sorry I didn't tell you that your engagement ring was part of the jewelry lifted from this store yesterday, but I couldn't. That detail is not information for public consumption."

He glared at me over Meg's head when he said the last, a reminder that I still hadn't explained how Meg learned her ring was missing. Maybe I could get out of here without mentioning Seth. Better that Troy learned of his involvement from Meg, not me.

"And yet you told Seth," Meg accused.

Troy's eyes widened. "Seth told you?"

"He told Daryl Anne and I happened to overhear."

Troy looked ready to explode. *So much for getting out of here unscathed.*

"Can you imagine," Meg said, her voice softer, the anger abating, but there was hurt in her words, "how it made me feel hearing that secondhand? *You* should have told me."

"I was hoping we'd recover the ring before you had to know." Troy lifted a finger to brush Meg's hair from her eyes. His gaze was tender. Full of love. "I wanted to spare you any distress, sweetheart."

Meg moved into his arms. I glanced longingly at the door, wanting to slip out and leave them alone, but they stood between me and the exit. I glanced at the floor, hummed in my head, trying not to listen to their cooing love talk. My gaze wandered to a wall clock. Crap. I was late. "Oh my God, I have to get to the bridal shop right now. Unless... Am I under arrest?"

"What?" Troy lifted his head from Meg's. "Oh. No. You can go. Just stay out of this investigation. Understand?"

"Absolutely," I lied, fingers crossed behind my back. No way

I could stop investigating this, not if he wanted to marry Meg and not if I wanted to clear Whitey of all suspicion, including my own.

As I scooted past Meg and Troy and hurried out into the hall, I heard Troy say, "Where did Daryl Anne get the idea there's a curse on my granny's ring?"

I picked up my pace, intending to leave without encountering anyone else who wanted a piece of me. I was in luck. I could see that Elton was outside with Whitey, discussing the security cameras.

"No kidding?" I heard Jenny say. I stopped in midflight. She was huddled at the end counter chatting with Elton Ring's daughter. The two shot apart as they sensed my intrusion. Veronica's face reddened, but Jenny remained calm. She gave me a bright smile. "Time to go?"

I nodded, saving my curiosity for the street. "We're late."

Stepping outside was like going from a soundproof box into a roaring carnival, cars and people everywhere I looked, happy chatter drowning the caw of the seagulls. Another day in expo hell. We both donned dark glasses against the glaring sun. I tugged Jenny to the crowded sidewalk, keeping well away from Elton and Whitey. We dodged shoppers, looky-loos, and locals making their way to various destinations. As we neared Blessing's Bridal, Jenny pulled up short.

"What?" I asked.

"Before we get swept up in the chaos of this day, I thought you might want to know what Ronnie told me about the robbery." Jenny smoothed her ponytail, her head tilting thoughtfully to one side. "Or is it burglary when someone steals from a store?"

"Ronnie?" I asked, steering the conversation back to the point.

"Veronica."

"I wasn't aware you knew Ver—er, Ronnie." Why hadn't she mentioned that fact before we entered the jewelry shop?

Jenny removed her sunglasses, pinching the bridge of her nose. "We met at Pre-Wedding Jitters. Lisa Marie introduced us and a couple of the other temps working the expo. We now meet there each morning for coffee before work to diss, er, discuss *interesting* customers and our employers."

I arched a brow at this last. A bee buzzed near my ear. I waved it away, along with any concern that Jenny was bad-mouthing my family. She was treated well, and if she dissed a customer or two, they probably deserved it. What had my full attention was this coffee klatch of hers. I was also kicking myself for not realizing sooner that she might've made friends with the other temps in town. In mystery books and detective shows, everyone underestimates what the servants and clerks overhear or know. These temps would be a source of information that might lead to my unveiling of a thief.

"So, who's in this coffee group?"

"Me, Ronnie, and…"

She rattled off names as I took note of where each worked, noticing one name that she hadn't included. "Not Hannah?"

Jenny's face clouded as she seemed to struggle for a polite way of saying, *Your cousin is weird.* She settled for, "Your relative is a bit of a loner."

I nodded in agreement. Then asked what I really wanted to know. "Did Ronnie volunteer the information about the, ah, jewel heist?"

Jenny shrugged. "We got to talking about this and that, and she sort of blurted it out."

"This and that?"

Jenny replaced her sunglasses and quirked her mouth. "She

doesn't want to work at the jewelry store. She wanted to go to art school in Los Angeles, but her father wouldn't pay for it. He made her take business classes online. Although he's more than willing for her to apply her creative juices to making an original jewelry line that he'll bankroll."

Veronica Ring, artist? I'd never imagined that shy ice princess had such a hidden talent. Or any hidden talent. In a small town like ours, keeping that secret would've been impossible. Even for Elton Ring. I wasn't sure I believed it.

On the other hand, I loved the idea of knowing someone who designed jewelry. "Is she going to do what her father wants?"

Jenny sighed. "Why can't parents embrace their children's dreams? Why do they look at their kids when they're babies and make up their minds about their kids' futures without even knowing if that's what their child will want when they grow up?"

I had no answer for that. I'd grown up not knowing anything but dressing other people and somewhere deep inside realizing and accepting that I'd one day be working at, or even owning, Blessing's Bridal. But I'd never resented my heritage. I wasn't so much forced into it as sucked into it. As far back as I could recall, I'd been fascinated by Gram's handwork, by the feel of the lace and chiffon, of satin and ribbons, of veils. And tiaras. Especially tiaras.

I said, "Inheriting your family business isn't always a bad thing."

Jenny's expression blanked for a quick second as if she couldn't relate on any level with that statement. "It is if you don't want it."

I didn't know her background but wondered if whatever went wrong between Jenny and her parents explained why they weren't involved in her upcoming wedding. I didn't ask. That little voice in my head was shouting at me like the white rabbit in *Alice in Wonderland*. "You're late...you're late..." Plus, I still didn't know what Jenny knew about the jewelry heist. I caught her elbow and got her moving. "What exactly did Ronnie tell you about the theft?"

"Did I mention that Ronnie and her boyfriend have secret plans to run off and get married as soon as the expo is over?" Jenny said without missing a beat or offering me any connection to what I'd asked.

I tamped down my impatience. "What did Ronnie say happened the day the jewels were stolen?"

"Oh, that. It was about the security system. The cameras inside haven't worked for six months. Her dad was too cheap to get them fixed. He said, 'Nothing ever happens in Weddingville.'"

Words Elton Ring will long regret. "I know. That's why Mr. Ring has Whitey installing a state-of-the-art security system."

We'd reached the back door of Blessing's Bridal. As we entered, Jenny said, "But don't you see? Ronnie was there. She had easy access to what was stolen. That's means and opportunity. And she's planning to run off and get married. She and her fiancé will need money. That's motive."

Chapter 9

The perfect wedding is in the details, the thief thought, running a finger down the edge of the cake knife, the serrated blade honed to the smoothness and sharpness of a razor. The solid gold gave the handle heft. It would make a formidable weapon, if the need arose. The irony was that it might still be in a showcase at that Bernice woman's shop if she hadn't been such a bitch to her customers and her staff. She'd been asking to be taught a lesson. She'd deserved to be robbed. But maybe that wasn't enough. Maybe, since she coveted this cake slicer, she should have it. Right through her mean heart. A smile played across the thief's face.

The knife slipped into the box alongside its mate, the metal shiny in the meager glow of the lamp. The thief's gaze shifted to the handful of rings, also on the table. The cops considered these stolen, but that wasn't so. They were only borrowed. *Something borrowed, something blue.* The edict was very clear. Everyone knew that.

Poking through the rings, the thief looked for the blue diamond, the eye-catching one that had led to *the borrowing.* Where was it? *The perfect symbol of our perfect love.* A red glint caught the thief's eye instead, as if it were speaking. This ring looked old. Maybe it was the band, or maybe the setting. The huge stone, a ruby perhaps, seemed to have depths like deep water, dark at its center, lighter near the edges. The thief peered closer, unable to look away, feeling a hypnotic pull as if it were somehow magical. Or cursed. A shudder went through the thief.

Go away, nasty red ring. You do not fit my wedding plans. The thief dropped the ruby ring into the to-be-returned pile. After all, you don't keep something you've only borrowed. The return was going to be more difficult now that the jeweler had updated his security system. That little glitch in plans would need to be worked out. *Hmm.*

As the thief considered the dilemma, the platinum blue-diamond ring revealed itself. *Aah. There you are, you magnificent beauty. Yes, details. Soon, my love, soon.*

Chapter 10

In the past two days," I told Meg as she slipped into the third tea-length dress she'd selected from the racks, "I've observed every size and shape of female in the hunt for the perfect wedding gown. I've come to the conclusion that most women don't know what looks best on their particular body."

"Very few women have any fashion sense," Meg agreed as I closed the back of the ivory lace gown that cinched in her waist. The bodice was heart-shaped, and the skirt flared slightly, giving the illusion of an hourglass. Her long, unruly curls spilled over the cap sleeves and onto her creamy skin. Tiny crystals had been woven throughout the fabric. My breath caught in my throat. She'd looked like a princess in the peachy Cinderella gown she'd worn for the wedding to Peter Wolfe, but in this gown, she might be a fairy queen. It was stunning. She was stunning.

She peered at herself in the mirror, her brow knit as if she didn't see what I was seeing. I feared it was her inner turmoil that blinded her to just how beautiful she looked. I hadn't brought up the ring, the curse, or whether or not she was going to marry Troy. She was here, trying on dresses, and that said more than words. But now I wondered if I should be her best friend and let her spill her guts.

However, she was apparently still mulling over the question about women and fashion. "You have to consider the role models most girls have growing up."

"Their mothers," I said automatically, thinking of my own, then twitching since Meg's mom had abandoned her when she was twelve. "Their aunts..."

"Teachers..." Meg smirked.

I burst out laughing, recalling our math teacher, Ms. Rhodes, who dressed like Dolly Parton. "Or their favorite celebrities, God forbid."

While I was fortunate to have had good style examples to learn from, Meg was born with a talent for clothes, makeup, and hair that I'd always envied. She'd been fast-tracking her way toward becoming a stylist to the stars when her life derailed. She might've lost that career and been forced to give up Hollywood for Weddingville, but she retained the natural talent and the skills she'd honed over the years. I'd hoped that once she was feeling like her old self again, she'd consider opening a salon here in town. It seemed, though, that she wasn't recouping as quickly as I'd hoped. Maybe if she had something to focus on that she was confident about...

I brought up the subject. "It's not as if a salon is my idea, Meg. It was all you talked about on the road trip home from Los Angeles." After her failed wedding and losing our dream jobs in L.A., we'd packed up our apartment and U-Hauled our belongings back here. It seemed so much longer than nine weeks ago.

"I don't know what I want to do yet, Daryl Anne." She looked equally undecided about the lacy gown, shifting this way and that and frowning at her image. This appointment had been her idea. Not mine. Somewhere inside, Meg was moving forward, even if she didn't recognize it yet.

"Come on, you can see yourself better in the three-way mirror." I led her out to the main room.

But someone else was already standing in front of the glass, my mother hovering nearby, a weariness around her eyes. It was the last customer of the day. Willa Bridezilla, Mom called her. This was the petite brunette's third visit to the shop. She was a perfect example of a woman who had no clue what style best suited her shape.

She took one glance at Meg's shimmery dress and declared, "That's what's missing. This dress needs bling. I want to shimmer, like her."

I swear Mom was stifling an eye-roll. I couldn't blame her. The dress didn't need bling; it needed a different bride. Someone tall and curvy.

"That dress doesn't need sparkles," Meg said as if she and Willa were old friends. "It's just too much dress for your tiny frame."

Willa recoiled as if Meg had called her an anorexic whore. "Excuse me? Who died and made you style goddess?"

"Diamonds wouldn't improve what you're seeing in the mirror," Meg answered as if she hadn't heard the retort. "You're not wearing that dress. It's wearing you."

I almost choked. Mom's face flushed pink and her mouth rounded, but no word or sound issued from her. I didn't know if she wanted to kiss Meg or ban her from the shop. But I sensed she was seeing dollar signs flushing down the toilet. This bride's budget allowed for one of the most expensive gowns Blessing's Bridal carried, and Willa was determined to spend that much or more. Or at least she had been until Meg spoke up. Now, it was anyone's guess, but if I were betting on it, I'd say, "Sale lost."

Willa scowled at her reflection. And I suddenly realized why she hadn't found a dress to give her that *special moment* every bride wants to feel when she puts on *the* gown. She wasn't emotionally vested in this purchase. Just monetarily. Why? Was she in a contest with her girlfriends to see who could spend the most money on their wedding? If so, I pitied her parents' pocketbook as well as the poor sap she was marrying.

"Bling." Willa pinned Mom with a look that said, *Hop to it, lady.*

"I suppose we could try a belt," Mom said, slipping into the back room.

I bit my tongue, my hands curling into fists at my sides. I was this close to ordering Willa to leave. The only thing stopping me was that I'd been raised to believe the customer was always right. Big Finn had taught Meg the same thing.

But recent life lessons had given Meg a new perspective on honesty, on what could come back and slap you in the face if you lied to yourself. Add that to her current anger stage of grief, and she couldn't restrain the need to set this bride straight. "That is a beautiful dress, but that voluminous skirt is swallowing you. Less is more, you know?"

The bride scowled at Meg, her eyes like slits, her nose wrinkled as if the tea-length gown Meg wore smelled like trash. "Yeah, I can see that appeals to you. But I can afford a whole dress."

My BFF's cheeks flashed pink dots, the first sign that turbo-temper had locked and loaded.

I almost shouted, "Fore!" to warn everyone to duck. Things were about to fly, and I wasn't sure the hurled items would only be words.

But Meg didn't holler; instead her voice was deceptively soft, and I held my breath as she said, "How much you spend on your dress won't ensure a happy marriage. And that dress not only looks awful on you, but you also can hardly maneuver in it. You'll trip going down the aisle."

The brunette huffed, muttered, "Bitch," and started toward Meg. Thank God Mom reappeared at that moment carrying a blinged-out belt. Willa gave a smug laugh and lifted her chin haughtily. Mom wrapped the belt around her and stepped back. Now attention was drawn to the belt, but not to the bride. Surely Willa could see that all eyes wouldn't be on her but on the dress.

"I'll take it," she said, startling us all.

After I lifted my chin off the floor, I had to tamp down my own irritation. This woman had ordered my mother around as if she were a servant and not the owner of a prestigious bridal shop, and she'd called my BFF a name when Meg was trying to make her see that the dress didn't suit her. If I had a speck of sense, I'd step away and say a silent "good riddance" to this bridezilla. But my conscience nagged like a bitter old hag. No matter how much I didn't want to deal with this customer again, I couldn't allow her to leave the shop with that dress as "the one."

Mom must have read my mind. She caught me by the shoulders and spun me away from Willa, speaking softly. "Sometimes you have to just take the money, Daryl Anne, and wish the bride well. This is one of those times."

I knew she was right, and yet, I was torn.

Mom brushed hair from her cheek, the strain of this sale evident in the lines at her eyes and mouth. "But you might apologize for Meg."

The suggestion raised my hackles. I dropped off the fence I'd been straddling. "No."

"No?" Mom stepped back, making her disapproval clear, even though she whispered it. "Then I'll apologize for her."

"No, you won't. We can't sell this woman that dress. You know I'm right. That Meg is right. What kind of reputation would we maintain if that was our practice?"

"What are you going to do?" Mom frowned, worry spreading through her eyes. "She's tried on every dress in the store in her price range."

"Not every dress." I strode over to the petite brunette. "Willa, a"—I rattled off the name of a coveted wedding dress designer—"arrived in a shipment today that is a sample size. Your size. It's a French lace and chiffon trumpet mermaid style with a scalloped neckline and a chapel train. It's a very special dress, and exactly right for your figure. We haven't even had time to take it out of the shipping box yet, but before you decide on this dress, I think you owe it to yourself to at least try that one on."

The brunette's ears twitched. I had her interest. She glanced at Mom. "How much is it?"

Mom found her composure with lightning speed. "Only a thousand more than your budget, but if you decide you love it, I'll take that thousand off."

"And throw in the veil?"

I tensed. A veil could run as much or more than a gown. Mom didn't hesitate, though. Happy brides meant free word-of-mouth advertising. Besides, I knew the dress was actually four thousand less than Willa's budget, which meant we could still come out ahead. But letting Willa think she was getting a deal was smart business. I silently applauded Mom's savvy.

"Can we do this now?" Willa asked. "I don't want to have to come back again tomorrow."

"Absolutely," Mom said. "I'll get the dress right away."

The dress had come in yesterday and was actually ready to be put out after the shop closed tonight. As Willa ducked into one of the dressing rooms, Mom gave me a thumbs-up and headed into the back room to get the gown.

"Will it be the one?" Meg asked.

"You know, I believe it will be. It's a stunner. Like you," I said, positioning her before the three-way mirror.

Meg glanced at herself, doubt still wavering in her big green eyes, but then something amazing occurred. Seth strode toward us carrying his mug, obviously headed for the coffeepot. He stopped in his tracks, his gaze locked on Meg. "Holy...Wow! Meg. You. That dress. Wow! Troy's going to be blown away."

I arched a brow, glad for the support but kind of taken aback. I wasn't sure I liked my guy's tongue hanging out when he looked at another woman, especially when that other woman was my best friend. I glanced back at Meg and realized that his compliment hadn't bounced off my best friend. Just the opposite. She blinked, then drew a sharp breath as if the blinders had been cleared from her eyes and she saw in the mirror what we all saw.

She gasped. "Oh my God, Daryl Anne, I love this dress. It's... it's amazing."

Tears welled in her eyes, and in mine, that *special moment* hitting both of us. I nodded, sniffling. "Seth is right. Troy O'Malley is one lucky guy."

Meg wiped her eyes and hugged me. "I'm the lucky one...to have such good friends. Thank you, Seth."

He shook his head, looking discomfited. "Just stating the truth."

"You think this one is the one?" I asked.

"Oh, yes, this is definitely my dress," Meg said, smiling. And I knew she was thinking what I was thinking. Those red satin slippers were going to be just the perfect complement to it. "Come on, help me out of this before I get mascara or makeup on it."

As we entered Meg's dressing room, Mom and Willa emerged from the other, the tiny brunette wearing the designer, trumpet-mermaid dress. She glided by us with ease and grace. Meg smiled at her, and I feared anything Meg said or did, even smile, would be taken wrong by Willa. I shoved Meg into the dressing room before she could blow the sale for Mom. But as soon as the door was shut, Meg said, "Did you see that dress? It's gorgeous on her."

"I know. Finally. Let's hope she agrees."

I helped Meg out of her dress, putting it carefully into a special garment bag as Meg slipped into the outfit she'd worn here, a short skirt and a pale green top that brought out her eyes. She was buckling her sandals when a cell phone rang. At first I thought it was mine, since Meg famously misplaced or couldn't find her own.

To my surprise, however, she actually had hers within reach, powered up and turned on. She pulled it from her skirt pocket. The ringtone was "Hawaiian Wedding Song." Her dad and new stepmom had spent their recent honeymoon in Maui. Since it seemed the wrong ringtone for Big Finn, I didn't figure it was announcing a call from her dad.

She said, "It's Zelda."

Duh. "I'll give you some privacy. I want to put this dress in Alterations." To ensure that nothing happened to it, like someone stealing it.

I left her to her phone call. Willa and Mom were still standing by the three-way mirror. Willa was saying, "I didn't think I'd like this much lace, but it's, ah, I feel so..." Her voice broke, as though she were choking up. Maybe having that *special moment* at long last? I could only hope.

I winked at Mom as I passed, but I heard Willa say, "I'll take it. At the special price you offered with the veil thrown in."

"I'll throw in a veil, but only if you choose one from this rack," Mom said, taking control again, her voice strong and sure.

A moment of hesitation, then Willa said, "Deal."

I proceeded to Alterations filled with relief. I placed Meg's dress on the reserved rack and tagged it with her name. Hannah appeared behind me. "You know that woman your mom just got the dress for? Willa?"

"Yes."

Hannah's blue eyes narrowed, the most animation I'd seen from her in years. "She's the one who stole Lisa Marie's fiancé."

"Are you sure?"

Hannah nodded. "She's doing all of her wedding shopping in town, rubbing Lisa Marie's nose in it."

Now I was sorry I hadn't let Willa leave with the dress that overwhelmed her. Really sorry. And she'd had the nerve to call my Meg a bitch. "The only consolation is that Lisa Marie's fiancé will deserve every miserable day of his marriage."

"Yep. See you tomorrow," Hannah said.

"Night." I went for coffee, hoping to run into Seth.

He'd started a new pot, the aroma uplifting, the small gesture thoughtful. He was always doing considerate things, like bringing in a new blend of coffee for us to try or ordering deli sandwiches if we were too busy to take a long lunch.

A smile gave away how happy I was to finally have a moment alone with him. "You know the way to a woman's heart, Quinlan."

"I'm only interested in one woman's heart, Blessing," he said, handing me a steaming cup. "I'm hoping you've forgiven me?"

"For?"

"Not admitting to Troy that I'm the one who told Meg about her ring being stolen."

"Oh, that," I said. "I wouldn't have told him either if he hadn't cornered me. He was pretty ticked off that you let the cat out of the bag."

"Yeah, he let me know. My ears are still singed." Seth grinned, and my insides began to heat with desire.

"Troy should have told her," I said, stepping toward Seth.

"How is Meg doing now?" He stepped closer to me.

We were almost touching. "I haven't discussed the ring, the curse, or anything related to the robbery with her. But on an up-note, she did find a dress."

"The one I just saw her in?" He leaned nearer my lips.

"Your reaction was the tipping point." My heartbeat thundered, and my eyelids fluttered shut in anticipation of his kiss. I could feel his breath feathering my face. A sigh escaped me.

"Daryl Anne!" Meg shouted, breaking into our intimate moment as if she were an overwrought child. "That was Zelda."

Regret flowed through me as I stepped back from Seth. He seemed as disappointed as I was about the interruption. Despite my best effort not to, I sounded disgruntled. "I know, Meg. I was in there when she called, remember?"

Meg didn't seem to notice my irritation. "Come on. We have to get to her shop."

"What?" I reared back, eluding her attempt to grab my hand. "Why?"

"Because the police are there."

"Damn," Seth said. "Was Zelda robbed, too?"

Meg was breathing hard. "I don't know what's going on. She was blubbering so hard, it took forever to get a few words out of her. I swear it sounded like she said she'd found a bunch of jewelry in her shop. Rings and things."

"But why would the police be there?" I asked, confused. Or probably still too annoyed to think straight.

Seth was quicker on the uptake. "You mean the jewelry stolen from the Ring Bearer?"

"Maybe," Meg said, looking uncertain while reaching for my hand again. "But that can't be right. Can it?"

Chapter 11

As we stepped outside into the waning afternoon, I wasn't sure if it was the adrenaline pumping through me that enhanced my senses or if it was the fresh air filling my lungs, but I felt alive again, as if the bridal shop were a stale-smelling jail from which I'd been freed. Or perhaps it was the sense that I was finally on the hunt again, the investigation progressing after being at a dead stall.

Whichever it was had my heart thudding and my feet moving at a clip. Shoppers were starting to drive away, parking spots emptying all along the street. The sun was still high in the sky on this July day, and the air held no sign of chill. I spied flashing lights a block off and the curious shuffling in that direction.

Meg and I picked up our pace, merging with the crowd gathering on the sidewalk around Zelda's wedding planning shop. I even saw Hannah there. Seth's long-legged stride had given him an unfair advantage, and he was a couple of car lengths ahead of us. He'd received a text just as we were leaving, and I suspected it was from Troy or Sheriff Gooden. We'd learn soon enough.

"Look," Meg said, pointing to something in the distance. "It's the Gossip Girls, right in front looking like kids about to watch a parade. How could they have beaten us here?"

"I don't know." *The town grapevine isn't high-speed Wi-Fi for crying out loud. At least not yet.*

"I'll bet one of them has a police scanner," Meg said, excusing herself as she tugged me past a strolling couple.

"Really?" My gaze flicked across the three snoop sisters. They were huddled, heads together like an elderly athletic team talking plays before hitting the field. "Which one, do you think?"

"Not Wanda," Meg said. "She bakes to the beat of Italian operas."

"True." No telling what her cannoli would taste like if she were listening in on police calls. I said, "Not Jeanette. Peace marcher, tree hugger, but not crime watcher."

Our gazes shifted to the senior with the flyaway gray hair, the grandmotherly body, the ants-in-her-pants, nervy one.

"Velda," Meg said.

I nodded. "She's always digging for the latest scoop."

"She's an instigator, too." Meg brushed her hair from her eyes, keeping her voice low as she elbowed people aside, clearing a path to the front door. "Excuse us, please. Coming through."

Folks who knew that Meg was Zelda's stepdaughter moved aside. Others, probably out-of-towners and gawkers, were less cordial or cooperative. We arrived on Zelda's doorstep ragged from worry and the July heat, only to be stopped in our tracks. By Troy.

He shook his head. "Oh, no you don't. You can't go in there."

"Zelda called me," Meg said, trying to get around her fiancé. "She wants me here. She is here, isn't she? Nothing's happened to her? Oh God, has something happened to her?"

Troy gently caught her upper arms. "She's fine, sweetheart. Just fine. But Sheriff Gooden is taking her statement at the moment, and no one's allowed in until he says so."

"Well, you let Seth go in," Meg said.

"He's working. Promise me, Meg, that you and Daryl Anne will stay right on this spot until I take care of dispersing the crowd."

Staying put was not on my agenda, especially with anticipation still coursing hot through my veins, and from the look on Meg's face, it wasn't on her agenda either. But I'd already almost been arrested two days ago at the jewelry store and that was filling me with a beach ball–sized hesitation.

"Break it up, folks," Troy told the crowd. "There's nothing to see. Nothing going on. No crime committed. No one hurt."

"Then why are you and the sheriff here?" Velda asked, standing her ground, her arms crossed over her sagging boobs. "It doesn't look like nothing to me, Troy O'Malley."

"Yeah, Troy, we saw Seth Quinlan and his camera go inside," Jeanette said, twisting her love beads. "Why was he allowed inside if nothing is going on? Huh?"

"Give us the scoop, Troy, and I'll give you a five percent discount on your wedding cake," Wanda wheedled.

Oh my God, Velda was rubbing off on Wanda worse than I'd thought.

Troy shook his head. "You ladies need to go on about your business. There's nothing going on here that concerns any of you."

"Okay, okay," Wanda said, waving her hand in the air. "Ten percent."

Troy jerked as a booming voice roared, "Zelda!"

The crowd went silent, shifting as a whole toward the sound of heavy footfalls coming up the sidewalk. Big Finn, looming ever closer like a redheaded Paul Bunyan, charged toward us. Onlookers cleared a path as wide as a crop circle, and Finn plowed through the opening, heading straight for the open shop door. "Zelda! Zelda?"

Troy beat him to the door, holding his hand up like a stop sign. "I'm sorry, Finn, you can't go in."

"Like hell I can't." His neck turning redder than his hair, Finn peered down at his soon-to-be son-in-law like a hawk about to gobble a starling.

But Troy—the boy who'd run off to the navy five years earlier, who might have been intimidated by his girlfriend's giant father—had been replaced by a tough, confident officer of the law. He wasn't backing down. He seemed to understand that if he allowed his future father-in-law to walk all over him in front of half the town, they would never manage a relationship built on mutual respect. "Finn, I'm sorry, this is a crime scene and off-limits while we investigate."

"Zelda!" Finn glared at the hand that Troy had clamped onto his lower arm.

"Your wife is fine. The sheriff is interviewing her."

"Remove your hand before I remove it for you."

"As long as you step back and stay outside."

I feared this would end badly. Two proud men, neither able to back down without losing face, locked in an unbreakable standoff. Meg seemed to size up the situation. She darted to her father's side. "Dad, please, Troy's only doing his job."

Big Finn's face softened as she wrapped her arms around him, and he pulled her into a hug. He'd been overly protective since Meg returned home—attention she'd lapped up like a cat long deprived of cream. But although he was holding his daughter, Finn's gaze never left the shop entrance. A tethered bull came to mind. There would be no holding him back once Zelda appeared.

"Zelda called me," he said to his daughter and to me. "She was crying so hard. I thought she was hurt."

"Troy swears she's fine," I said, having no reason to think Troy would lie.

While Finn and Meg talked quietly, I assessed what I knew about this. From the disjointed conversation Meg had had with Zelda, it seemed she was hysterical. Sobbing, blurting out something about the police and jewelry. I frowned. I knew Zelda could be flighty at times, but she wasn't the type for a complete meltdown. Her job required nerves of steel and an alligator hide. Every day she had to placate demanding brides and juggle critical mothers and budget-minded fathers. She had to regularly disarm jealous entourages intent on negating every choice a bride made. All that while also handling several weddings at once.

Not much shook this woman. No wonder Meg and Big Finn were rattled. But it wasn't like she'd found a dead body sprawled across boxes of invitations. No. She'd found some jewelry in the bathroom. So why would that throw the wedding planner into such a tizzy? Of course, the first conclusion I leaped to was that she'd found the jewelry stolen from the Ring Bearer. But since the police hadn't released any details about the stolen items, how would Zelda know that that was what she'd found?

I stared at the Gossip Girls, trying to work the problem through, and I kept coming back to the same answer. There was only one way she could know. Meg's ruby ring had to be among the items she'd found. Was it? God, I hoped so. For the sake of Meg's sanity.

But seriously, even that wouldn't have thrown Zelda into a crying jag. That was the puzzle. I studied the front of the shop, visualizing the interior. She didn't have a security system in place. No cameras with footage the police could view for potential suspects. No need for such things. My gaze shifted over the crowd that had grown, not diminished. Was the thief here now? Watching? Reveling in the excitement he or she had created? I spotted my cousin again, and a shiver swept through me.

"Was she robbed, do you think?" Velda said, standing at my elbow.

I blinked, staring down at her and then at her faithful companions. Talk about a mischievous entourage. They had devilment in their eyes. When had they managed to get this close? That'd teach me for getting lost in thought.

"I doubt it. She doesn't carry much inventory. Nothing thief-worthy."

"Yeah," Jeanette said. "Not like your bridal shop. Billie says you've got thousands of dollars tied up in all those wedding gowns and veils and tiaras and things."

Hundreds of thousands. I kept the thought to myself. How did I know who might overhear and take that as an invitation to rip off Blessing's Bridal? The thought made me ill. And I was back to square one. Why had Zelda become hysterical over some found jewelry?

"I heard someone knocked Zelda out, and she was found on the bathroom floor," Velda said. Beads of sweat dotted her upper lip, drawing my eye to the mustache I'd never noticed until this moment. Meg really needed to open a beauty salon and offer facial waxing.

"If she'd been knocked out, there would be an ambulance." Right? Meg hadn't said anything about Zelda being knocked out. "Troy says she's fine. Just fine."

"I heard she caught someone trying to rob her till." Wanda's brows were knit, her expression irate. I figured anyone trying to rip her off risked being conked with a rolling pin, a heavy-duty marble one. But that was only a guess.

"I heard she tied him up," Jeanette said, fingering a peace sign pendant that hung on a brass chain. The touch of glee in her voice was not only surprising, but also disturbing. Apparently her sense of goodwill had limited reach.

"I also heard she locked someone in the bathroom," Velda declared, her breath smelling like rotten fish. She was daring me to contradict her silly statement.

How could I resist that challenge? "If she'd done that, Troy would have the perp cooling his or her heels in the squad car by now."

The Gossip Girls' heads shifted in unison toward the police sedan hugging the curb. The vehicle was empty.

"Huh." Velda sniffed, scowling at me. "You should be a stand-up comedian, Daryl Anne Blessing."

I bit the inside of my cheek and turned my attention back toward Zelda's shop. My mind reverted to puzzling over the jewelry situation and why Zelda was so unhinged. Had she realized she'd been alone with a thief who might very well have been armed and dangerous? Or did Zelda perhaps know who'd used her bathroom and that was why she was upset?

The waiting to find out was causing my nerves to twitch. If the thief were known, an arrest would be imminent, and my investigation would be ended before it had really begun. But the community and shop owners would breathe easier. Even me. And yet, disappointment curled through me. I mean, of course I'd be happy for Meg if Granny O'Malley's ring had been recovered. No more curse to worry her.

And on a selfish note, that would simplify my main task as maid of honor.

Seth appeared in the doorway, squinting against the sunlight like a miner emerging from a pit. He spotted me and started in my direction, and I forgot why I was here. It was that loose-jointed walk, the camera bumping his hip with every step, that male swagger that came natural to him. His mouth was lifting slightly at the corners, a silent message to me. My blood seemed to warm, and my mouth watered.

Sheriff Gooden emerged, caught Troy's eye, and barked, "I thought I told you to disperse this crowd."

"I've been trying, sir." Troy spread his arms in frustration. "They just won't leave."

Sheriff Gooden was around the age my dad would be if he hadn't died too young from a bad heart. He was well thought of in this county, but I'd encountered his take-charge attitude in the past, and I recognized that assertiveness in his bearing now. He glanced toward the milling townsfolk, especially the Gossip Girls.

"There is nothing to see here. I suggest you all be on your way. Go on now. Get going." He waved his hands as if shooing away birds. Wanda, Jeanette, and Velda didn't budge. He narrowed his eyes. "Do I have to haul you ladies in for loitering?"

"You wouldn't dare," Wanda said. "I'm a respected business owner in this community."

"Try me," Sheriff Gooden said, not brooking any argument.

"Well, I never," Velda said as the three women stomped off.

Big Finn and Meg hurried inside to check on Zelda, closing the door and shutting out everyone else, including me. A moment later, the crowd had thinned to Seth, me, and Troy. Both men knew what was going on. I did not. Curiosity twisted my insides.

I knew they'd probably just shut down my questions, but I had to ask, "Is it true? Did Zelda find the missing jewelry in her shop?"

Before Troy could tell me it was none of my business, Meg

came running out. She rushed to Troy's side. "Zelda says my ring was with the jewelry she found."

Troy pressed his lips together and nodded, looking as if he'd hoped that Zelda wouldn't reveal that detail to Meg.

"Where is it? I want it back. Now."

Troy shook his head. "Sweetheart, you have to understand—"

"Understand what?"

"I can't give you the ring now…," Troy said, his voice trailing off.

Meg sighed. "Okay. Sure. It needs to be logged in, but first thing tomorrow, right?"

"Ah, yeah." Troy lifted his hat and scratched his head. "Not then either."

"Why not?" Meg was tapping her foot, barely restraining her temper if the white around her lips was any indication. I got a modicum of pleasure in the silent stare she was giving him. It was as good as any he'd given me.

"Well," Troy blustered, "first we have to find the person who stole it."

"First? What?" Meg blinked hard and fast, imitating the victim of a dozen camera flashes. "But what if you never find him?"

Troy swallowed so hard his Adam's apple bobbed. "It's evidence in an open case."

"Oh my God. That damned curse." Meg threw her hands up and wailed, "That's it. I'm done. I love you, Troy O'Malley. I guess I always have, and I always will. But I won't risk making your life a misery. The engagement is off. I can't marry you. I won't."

With that, she ran off toward Cold Feet Café as if a pack of dogs were chasing her.

Sheriff Gooden clamped Troy on the shoulder. "Looks like you escaped by the skin of your teeth, son. That one's a little off kilter. Imagine what your life would be like if you had married her." He gave a little shudder, then ambled off toward his squad car. "Yep, lucky to be rid of her."

I watched him depart, wishing my anger felt like spear gun barbs drilling into his back. Narrow-minded jerk. He'd just given me another reason to vote for his opponent in the next election, no matter who ran against him.

"Don't listen to Gooden," Seth told Troy. "Meg's just upset. It's been an upsetting day for her family. She said she loves you. She'll come around."

Troy's blue eyes were as empty as a drained glass, his body limp. I wasn't sure he was hearing Seth.

I gripped his lower arm, catching his glance. "Troy, listen to Seth. Meg's overly emotional right now. Irrational. She's still grieving, trying to come to terms with all the sudden changes that have occurred in a very short span of time. We all need to be patient with her."

We also had to figure out what that damned curse was and remove it from the ring. Easy-peasy, right? *Anyone know an Irish Traveler with "the sight" who specializes in the exorcism of bad juju? If so, call me at 1-800-desperate maid of honor.*

Chapter 12

I needed a drink, a lift to my spirits that only somewhere fun and lively could provide. Seth felt the same. We opted for the Last Fling, a tavern several blocks out of town just beyond the residential areas. Once a lumberman's lodge, the log building backed against a stand of Douglas fir, new growth that had replaced the original trees used as material to build this place. I hadn't been here since Meg's mom was abducted from the parking lot, strangled, and dumped from a cliff not far from here. Walking up to the door sent shivers through me.

Except for the name, the outside screamed lumberjack and biker gang hangout. Inside, the baseball caps that used to hang from the ceiling had been replaced by garters in a rainbow of colors, including one black garter.

The drink menu featured several cocktails with bridal themes. The one named after this establishment contained four different liquors, including a 100-proof Vodka. I'd heard tell that, after downing one drink, a person could forget their own name. I'd never been tempted to try it. But then, when it comes to booze, I'm a lightweight. Two glasses of wine is pretty much my limit...per week.

I ordered a Honeymoon Sweet, which was an Irish coffee, easy on the Irish, heavy on the cream. Seth had a Groomsman lager, a local brewery favorite that this bar had on tap. I stirred whipped cream with my straw, then took a sip. The bartender had ignored my "easy on the Irish," and I wasn't sorry. Not at that moment anyway. I might be later. I hadn't realized how much I craved something bracing until it started working through my system, reducing my tension.

"Five pennies for your thoughts, Blessing," Seth said, and like every time before, it drew a smile from me.

I met his warm gaze with one of my own. If only I could concentrate on the two of us and shut out the rest of the world, but no matter how much I wanted that, it seemed impossible. At the moment, my mind felt as if all its content had been put in a sack, floured, and fried. Shake 'N Bake brains. Nothing connected, nothing made sense. Just a jumble of questions without answers or resolutions.

I licked cream from the edge of my mouth, Seth's gaze following the movement of my tongue as his cocoa-colored eyes darkened to a rich, smoldering chocolate. I tried to ignore the wicked, delicious sensations tumbling through me, but I noticed a throaty edge to my voice. "I'm afraid if I let you offer up that penny, you'd end up like someone on that reality show where they bid for storage units."

He frowned. "Huh?"

"You'd regret buying what's revealed."

He laughed. "I can afford the nickel."

I sipped my drink. Why did it feel like telling him would be opening a Pandora's box, since there wasn't much, if anything, either of us could do about it? Not at the moment anyway. But he wouldn't believe a lie. I sucked at lying. I gave in and said,

"I didn't want to worry Troy, but I'm really concerned about Meg. She's on the edge of tipping over. I can't let that happen. But I don't know how to help her. She really believes that ring is cursed."

He looked at his beer for a long second, then at me with a serious gaze. "Is it?"

I don't know what I expected him to say, but certainly not that. "What?"

"Is the ring cursed?"

My brows seemed to lift into my hairline. "You believe in... curses?"

"Why not? I don't know that they don't exist."

I sank back onto the bar stool. *Who is this man? The knight in shining armor, I understand. But this?* I didn't know what to think. Then again, I reminded myself, Seth viewed the world through a different lens, catching on camera things that weren't always seen by the naked eye. Perhaps this broadened his perspective on possibilities. This new discovery about him felt like finding a treasure where none was expected. At every turn, I liked this man more and more. "You're a surprise a minute, Quinlan," I said, then took another sip of my drink.

"Is that a bad thing?" He looked worried. "Something you don't want to be around?"

I supposed for some women it might be, but I adored the idea of a man with an open mind, even if it was open to the weird or the unproven. Left to my own devices, I would trudge through life taking too much at face value, while skipping over all that might be. Meg, and now Seth, made me open my eyes to what my narrowed vision missed. My world would be a sadder, smaller place without their influences. "No, it's quite wonderful, actually." I touched his knee.

He leaned toward me. "Careful, Blessing, I might have to collect on that rain check you owe me."

It's about time, I thought, licking more cream from my mouth, noticing him noticing, and not regretting the heat that filled his gaze. "Fine by me."

"Damn. I wish I'd offered you a drink at my place instead of the Last Fling."

"What've you got to offer me there that I can't get here?" I asked in a low, whispery voice. Seth didn't speak, just gave me a suggestive look that sizzled my nerves and curled my toes.

"Ooh... my favorite."

* * *

Sonny greeted us at the door with his leash in his mouth. Seth laughed. "Are you happy to see me, buddy, or just wanting your walk?"

"Both," I said, squatting to give the yellow lab a hug and getting my face laved for that good deed.

"Not tonight, pal," Seth told the dog, letting him out into the fenced backyard. If Sonny was disappointed, he didn't show it. "I really have to get the new doggy door installed. This one was fine when Sonny was a pup, but obviously he's outgrown it."

Seth turned and nearly rammed into me. I'd been standing that close. *Have I mentioned that patience isn't my thing?* It seemed as if I'd waited all my life for him to notice me, to acknowledge me, to be interested in me. I'd finally decided it was a pipe dream, a fantasy I'd never realize. And then the impossible happened. And now that it had, I was done with waiting.

I didn't even try to hide my feelings. But nothing prepared me for his reaction. He stopped as if seeing me for the first time, and the awe in his gaze humbled me. I wasn't deserving of such adoration. And yet, I couldn't look away. Without touching me, he had my every nerve tingling. *My first tantric sex?* I had no clue. I wasn't sure what tantric sex involved, but I'd heard there was no touching. Just almost touching. My senses were wholly engaged, anticipation raging hot through me.

Seth seemed equally unnerved. Excited. Good. I wanted this experience to be like no other for both of us.

He said, "Er, I have a bottle of wine in the fridge. Some kind of white. Or beer?"

"No thank you."

"I have some hard stuff…" He pointed toward a cupboard.

"The only thing hard I want is you."

He smiled, his voice going gravelly. "And here I was thinking you were thirsty."

"I didn't come here for a beverage. All I want to drink is you."

His gaze lighted from deep within. "Talk about someone who's full of surprises, Blessing."

He pulled me to him and kissed me hard, as if he'd been waiting forever to do just that. His fierce possession of my mouth pulled a tiny yelp from me. I drew him closer, crazy to rush, all the while fearing it would be over too soon. I didn't want it to ever be over. He pulled me tighter still. There was no mistaking how eager he was to collect that rain check.

On a breathless note, I asked, "Are you happy to see me, Quinlan, or just wanting to go for a walk?"

He gave an animal growl. "What do you think?"

"A walk?" I teased.

He laughed and scooped me off my feet. "The only walk you're going on is to my bedroom."

Don't ask me what his bedroom looked like. My usual attention to detail wasn't interested in décor. All I saw was a huge bed, lots of pillows, and Seth. Panic and insecurity set in. What if he found me wanting? What if he had secret cameras hidden in this room? Would I be in a sex tape that went viral? *God, Daryl Anne. Listen to yourself. You're as delusional as you are anxious.*

And why wouldn't I be? I wasn't a seductress; I didn't have carnal moves or techniques. The few sexual encounters I'd enjoyed over the years were more of a disappointing, slam-bam, thank-you-ma'am variety. I didn't recall ever before feeling this emotionally invested, this passionate pull to have a man touch me. Everywhere. In ways I'd only imagined.

But what if I sucked at sex? Hah. My stomach pinched. Even puns didn't allay my nervousness. I reminded myself that guys often said, *Bad sex is better than no sex.* As a consolation, it didn't reassure me. My worry, I realized, was easily read in my expression.

Seth touched my cheek. "Ah, Blessing, why the frown? Have you changed your mind?"

Changed my mind? Hell, no. Even if I was the worst partner he'd ever had, I was not missing out on sex with Seth. *Nuh-uh. No way.* I reached for his shirt and started tugging it loose from his jeans. He made a happy noise. And then, finally, he was touching me, his hands peeling away my clothes like a nervous, clumsy schoolboy, the eagerness on his face echoing the need speeding through me.

As he reached to unhook my bra, he said, "I want to see every inch of you, Blessing, but if you're uncomfortable with that, I'll turn off the light."

God, he was the most thoughtful man. And I wanted to see all of him, too. "I've waited too long for this to do it in the dark."

"Oh, yeah?"

"Yeah," I said, leaving it vague and losing my next thought in another of his mind-stealing kisses. And then we were both naked, and neither of us needed pennies to know what the other was thinking.

* * *

The next day, Meg took one look at my face and declared, "Oh my God, Daryl Anne Blessing, you're positively glowing. And giddy. If I run into Seth, will he be wearing that same sappy grin?"

My cheeks heated at how he'd looked when I left him an hour or so ago, still snuggled in his bed, a hint of a smile on his sleeping face, and I had to stifle a huge sigh. "Hush, Meg. Someone will hear you," I said as we settled at a table in Pre-Wedding Jitters.

"Are you kidding? I want details."

"No." Impossibly, my face felt hotter.

Meg chuckled at my scowl.

"I don't kiss and tell."

"Maybe not, but you wouldn't be this rosy if all you did was kiss."

She had me there. But I wasn't going to discuss the details of last night with anyone, except maybe Seth. It was ours to treasure.

"Ah, just the two I was hoping would show up," Lisa Marie greeted us. Meg had been getting this response from everyone we'd encountered today. The question from one and all: Why were the police at Zelda's yesterday?

"Is your mom still gone Elvis hunting?" Meg deflected. She wasn't allowed to discuss what had gone on at Zelda's with anyone. Although I intended to get her to make an exception in my case.

Lisa Marie said, "The King Sisters group has taken off for another state. Not sure when Mom will return."

I caught a hint of sadness beneath the bright smile she was offering us. I'd probably feel the same if my mother chased after deceased icons.

Lisa Marie didn't ask about Zelda but instead said, "Daryl Anne, I heard a rumor that a certain fiancé-stealing bridezilla bought a wedding dress in Blessings late yesterday. Is it true?"

I gulped and tried a deflection of my own. "We sell a lot of wedding gowns to brides who might qualify as bridezillas, but most probably aren't fiancé-stealers. Could you be more specific?"

"Skinny runt. Muddy brown hair. Named Willa." The black ice in Lisa Marie's gaze could freeze the steam floating off a cup of hot espresso.

"Oh my God, Dillon is marrying that little bitch?" Meg said, her eyes bugged.

"You've met her?" Lisa Marie curled her lip.

Meg gave a shudder. "Unfortunately."

I squirmed in my seat, really, really regretting that I'd helped Willa find her *special feeling* dress, instead of something that made her look as ugly outside as she was inside. I was pretty sure my face reflected pure guilt. "Er...ah...we did have a customer named Willa, and she did buy a dress. I'm sorry. I didn't know about her...and you...and Dillon."

Meg's eyes held a silent accusation. *Why didn't you tell me?*

"I could kill her," Lisa Marie murmured, the words sending a shock through me.

Meg clamped a hand over Lisa Marie's. "As someone who's just been through something similar, let me tell you, hon, you're better off. A guy who marries for money will spend every day of his life paying for it. Let me tell you, having met his future ball and chain, Dillon's going to be one sorry sap."

"Thanks." Lisa Marie gave Meg a quick hug. "I know you're

right. I know I shouldn't let her get to me, but every time I hear of somewhere else she's been in town, I want to do her bodily harm."

The drive-through bell sounded, sending Lisa Marie back behind the counter and leaving Meg and I staring at each other. Meg said, "When did you find out about Willa and Dillon?"

I explained that Hannah had told me after we'd already helped Willa find a better dress, and how much I wished we had let her buy the one that made her look like a life-sized pom-pom. "I feel so bad for Lisa Marie."

"She's better off. She might not know it now, but she will eventually."

"And what about you?" I asked Meg. "Is the wedding on or off?"

"Off."

"Then you really don't want to marry Troy."

Meg made a little unhappy laugh. "Ironically, I do want to marry him, but I can't. Not without that ring." I watched her poke a straw into the lid of her latte. Sadness wafted from my best friend and filled me with helplessness.

I sighed. This situation was unacceptable. Curse be damned. I couldn't allow Meg to have two failed weddings under her belt. That would make me a two-time loser as maid of honor, and I didn't want that on my record. "What exactly is the curse on Granny O'Malley's ruby ring anyway?"

Meg planted her lips on the straw, avoiding eye contact for several seconds as she enjoyed the iced coffee drink. Finally, she lifted her gaze. "I'm not sure. I mean, I was fifteen, after all, when she told me about it."

"Yes, I know. And at fifteen, girls are very impressionable. A story like that would end up etched in your memory."

I waited while she closed her eyes, a frown furrowing her brow, her mouth scrunching as if she was some deep thinker considering the secrets of the universe. Frustration and impatience got the better of me. "What, Meg?"

She leveled those big green eyes at me. "I don't remember. Honest. I recall the day and even what Granny O'Malley was wearing."

Like that was a revelation. "Even I recall what she wore and I wasn't there. Black from head to toe like the witch in *Wizard of Oz* and a wrist full of tingling, Gypsy bracelets, right?"

"Yes," Meg said sheepishly. "But honestly, I don't know what she said. It's like I can see her in my mind, holding the ring in her palm. Her lips are moving, but there's no sound. No words."

"Geesh." I sank back in my chair and considered the problem. "Someone in the family must know about the curse. It's the kind of thing that's passed from generation to generation."

"Troy doesn't know what it is either."

That gave me pause. She hadn't just dreamed up a curse, had she? Her subconscious trying to tell her not to marry Troy? I wasn't sure I should suggest that, but then I remembered what Seth had asked me. "Is there really a curse on the ring?"

Meg blanched. "You thinking I'm lying?"

"No. I'm wondering if Granny O'Malley lied to you."

"Why would she?"

"She was always saying weird things." It wasn't much of an answer, but I wouldn't put it past the old woman to have embellished or made up a story to make the ring seem more interesting. How did we find the truth now? I wanted to bang my head on the table. Of course there couldn't be a simple solution. If there were, it wouldn't involve Meg.

The coffee shop's door opened and Jenny, our temp, bustled

in trailed by the temp from Something Old, Something New, whom I'd never met, and Violet Pringle, whose mother owned the Flower Girl. Violet had been one of the bridesmaids for Meg's earlier wedding.

She came over to us, chatted for a second, then turned to Lisa Marie and said, "We're having a sale on yellow roses today. I need a quadruple shot, caramel venti, iced."

Lisa Marie set to work. "I love yellow roses. Save me a bouquet. I'll come by during the afternoon lull."

As she moved off, leaving Meg and me alone again, I was still mulling over how to discover the truth about the cursed ring. Troy didn't believe there was a curse, but despite not recalling what the curse was, Meg believed it with all her heart. There was only one thing I could think to do. Go over Troy's head. "Meg, I think we should ask Troy's mother about the curse. She has to know. After all, she chose not to accept that ring when she married Troy's dad."

A gleam of hope appeared in Meg's eyes, and the corners of her mouth tilted up ever so slightly. "That's a great idea. If we go now, we should be able to catch Gwen before she leaves for work."

"Great." I shoved back my chair, grabbed my to-go cup, and followed Meg out the door and into the promising morning. I should've gone straight home, showered, and changed in order to be ready when the bridal shop opened for business in an hour, but I was in maid-of-honor mode, where curses took priority over customers.

Chapter 13

Curse?" Gwen O'Malley's face contorted, and she burst out laughing. "Oh my, that's hilarious. Where did you ever get such an idea, Meg?"

"From Granny O," Meg said. "She told me when I was fifteen."

We were in the O'Malleys' spotless kitchen, a cozy room that made me picture long, lazy mornings over coffee and newspapers and conversations about nothing more important than which seeds to plant in the veggie garden out back. The sunny yellow walls and white cabinets and trim were as welcoming as a morning breeze on a warm day. I inhaled the lingering scents of fried eggs and bacon, and a hint of bleach, and wished we were here to chat about coffee and home gardens. But we weren't.

My attention shifted back to Troy's mother. Gwen was smirking, barely able to contain her amusement. "What kind of curse did she tell you was placed on the ring?"

Meg closed her eyes and inhaled, probably weighing how "hilarious" her future mother-in-law would find the answer. She seemed about lose it, her lower lip caught in her teeth. I feared she'd bite a chunk of skin off if she got more distressed.

"That's just it," I said in an effort to calm my anxious bride, praying Gwen had something to tell us that would also calm me. "Meg can't recall the particulars of the curse. We were hoping that you'd remember."

Gwen studied me as if she thought we were pranking her. "You're serious about this?"

As serious as the thousand dazzling rhinestones on your jacket. She thought the idea of a curse was odd, and yet, she seemed to have a Bedazzler fetish. Okay, so it was understandable. After all, she worked in Gig Harbor for a craft shop. But still...Note to self: Don't let Gwen anywhere near Meg's wedding gown. "This isn't a joke," I assured her.

"Really?" She remained unconvinced.

"Really," Meg said.

Skepticism pulled Gwen's brows together, creating twin lines at the top of her nose. "Even so, why is this so important that you're here this morning risking us all being late for work?"

I locked gazes with my best friend. It wasn't my place to tell Gwen that the wedding hinged on this. That was up to Meg. Meg shook her head, gesturing with her hand that I should just tell Gwen. I shook my head harder. I had to draw the line somewhere. After all, I didn't even believe in curses. Much. I said, "Tell her."

"Okay." Meg huffed. She lifted her hair off her neck and let it drop back to her shoulders. Then speaking so softly that I could hardly hear her, she said, "Unless the curse is removed from that ruby ring, I'm not going to marry Troy."

"Excuse me?" Gwen almost toppled off her stool. "Did you say you're not going to marry my son unless a curse is removed from Granny O's ring?"

I swear Meg was holding her breath. I didn't think she could find the air to get those words out again. I answered for her, "Yeah, that."

Every trace of humor disappeared from Gwen's regal face, replaced by a deer-in-the-headlights mien. "But you must marry Troy. He loves you. We've got an appointment to taste cake samples at the Wedding Bakery."

If only that logic would fix this mess. "Meg loves Troy, too, but this curse has her pretty freaked out."

"Well, if it's any consolation, now I'm freaked out, too." Gwen straightened her jacket and reached out to cover Meg's hand with her own. "But I assure you, Meg, sweetie, there is no curse. You've just got a bad case of cold feet."

Meg frowned. "What?"

"Girls, I have to run. I'll be late if I don't leave right this minute. And I am never late."

"But...," Meg said.

"No, no. I don't want to hear any more about this. You just concentrate on my darling son and your future together. It's going to be wonderful." She led us out of the house to her car, got in, started the engine, and waved to us as she drove off.

Meg and I stood next to the garage, silent. I couldn't speak for her, but I was feeling as numb as my jaw after a visit to the dentist. "What just happened?"

"We got the fast shuffle," Meg said, sounding desolate. "She's really good at brushing aside anything she doesn't want to hear or deal with. She could make a mint selling those rose-colored glasses."

I wasn't sure if that was a good trait in a mother-in-law or if it would present Meg with a lot of headaches over the years. "Now what?"

She shrugged, sinking onto a nearby concrete retaining wall

that ran the length of the driveway. "Now nothing. It's over. I'm destined to be an old maid."

Oh, brother. I sat beside her. After last night, I was feeling way too good about my chances of not living life celibate, and I wasn't about to have that be my best friend's fate either. "There must be something or someone who knows about curses and how to remove one."

"I Googled curses on engagement rings. A gazillion sites popped up. It would take years to read all the articles."

"Without any guarantee we'd find the curse that's on your ruby ring," I finished for her. "We could narrow down the Google search if we knew what the curse was."

Guilt spread across Meg's face. She thought this was her fault, when in fact, circumstances had just conspired against her. Again. She said, "It has something to do with weddings or marriages, but beyond that, it could be any kind of curse. What if trying to remove the wrong curse makes it worse?"

This was crazy. Why couldn't Meg just get engaged like any normal person and proceed without one glitch after another? Like a foreshadowing, a dark cloud floated across the sun, momentarily robbing the bright light around us. Although it wasn't cold, I shivered. What were we going to do? I didn't want Meg to know that I was as disillusioned as she was. I only wanted her to be happy again. Like she'd been before coming back to Weddingville.

"Psst."

"Did you say something?" I asked Meg.

"No. I thought it was you."

"Psst."

We both glanced toward the back door of Joe and Gwen's house. The door was cracked open, and Joe O'Malley was leaning out. "Is Gwen gone?"

We hopped off the retaining wall, swiping at the rear of our running pants. I said, "She left a couple minutes ago."

"Good." He gestured for us to come into the kitchen again. We hurried over and back inside. He was dressed in a white T-shirt, blue jeans, and white socks, as if he'd been getting ready for work but stopped to speak to us. He strode to the counter, lifted a thermos, and filled a mug. "Coffee?"

We declined. We were both at least ten minutes late to work and very much in need of showers and a change of clothes after our run. But as anxious as I was to be heading to the bridal shop, I also wanted to hear what Joe wanted.

He gestured us toward the table, and as I sat, I noticed a daub of shaving cream dotted one cheek. "I overheard what you were discussing with Gwen," he said, taking a seat at the table. "She doesn't know anything about the ring because I never told her about it. Besides, look around. Gwen likes putting her own stamp on things."

I hadn't noticed before that the toaster cover, the tea cozy, and the place mats were all homemade. I wasn't sure how they'd missed being Bedazzled, but then again, Gwen gave craft classes on all sorts of things.

Joe said, "Accepting a ring that had belonged to someone else would never do for her."

"Is your grandmother's ring cursed?" I asked, tired of getting the runaround.

"No. Not at all." His answer didn't ease the pained look in his eyes. "You have to understand that my grandmother was from another place and time. Illness forced her to come live in Weddingville with my parents and siblings. She'd never lived in just one place. Her home was wherever the Travelers were. She was lost and lonely, and her mind was slowly slipping away. Alzheimer's. Not a curse."

"But," Meg said, her tone measured as she carefully selected her words, "she was lucid the day she told me about the ring."

"Was she? Think back with the caveat of what I've just told you." Joe turned sympathetic eyes on his would-be daughter-in-law. "Doesn't it make you look at what she said differently?"

Meg let the words settle over her, and I saw a shifting in her body language, as if tension were slipping from tight muscles and worry dissolving in its wake. "I suppose..."

"Ah, that's great." Joe grinned, his handsome face echoing his son's great looks. He stood up, our signal that it was time to go. "Now let's not hear any more nonsense about you not marrying my son. You two belong together. Just pick out a ring and forget about the one Granny O gave Troy for his bride."

A moment later, we found ourselves outside again, standing in the O'Malleys' driveway. I clasped Meg around the shoulders. "See, no curse. Just the ramblings of a woman with dementia."

It was late; even three blocks from town I could hear the commotion going on. My phone vibrated in my pocket for the tenth time. I stopped ignoring it. I had four texts from Gram and two from Mom. My stomach dipped. She'd had to take my early morning appointment, and I needed to be at the bridal shop in twenty minutes to take her appointment. I told Meg, and we started jogging toward town.

We'd gone around two blocks when Meg said, "It's so sad, isn't it?"

I gaped. She couldn't be serious. "You're sad because there's no curse?"

She shook her head, puffing as we ran. "That all us kids thought that poor lonely old woman was a witch. Kids can be so cruel."

Including me. Guilt and shame pounded the pavement with

my every footfall. I'd always been convinced Granny O was somehow evil. Now, looking back as an adult armed with facts, I realized all the signs of dementia were there; I'd just been too young to recognize them. "I'm sure that's the only reason you believed what she told you about the ring being cursed."

Meg nodded, then suddenly stopped in her tracks, catching my arm and pulling me up short. "Oh my God, Daryl Anne. I remember. I know what she said about the ring."

Of course she'd remember now, when it didn't matter. She didn't expand, just stood there with an array of emotions flickering across her face like credits at the end of a movie. I bumped her arm. "Are you going to make me guess?"

Meg's gaze pinned me. "She might not have been a witch, and she might've been losing her mind, but even Joe will tell you that she did have 'the sight.'"

I'd never told Meg, but Billie believed that, too. I just nodded, waiting for her to continue.

"She said that she'd seen the future and that if I wed Troy with her ruby ring, we'd have a long and happy union. If he slipped any other ring on my finger, however, we were doomed."

"This is amazingly good news." I smiled, wondering why she wasn't smiling with me.

"No, it's not. Have you forgotten the ring is in police custody, evidence in a crime that has not been solved?" Tension seemed to grab hold of Meg's muscles with renewed vigor. "I can't marry Troy until the Weddingville burglar is caught and tried and my ring is no longer evidence. The court system is so slow, even if the thief is caught right away, it could be years before he or she is convicted. Or longer, if the robberies go unsolved."

Oh crap. She was right. "Maybe if you and Troy explain the situation to Sheriff Gooden, he'll relent and release the ring."

"Yeah right. 'Cause he's sympathetic to young lovers."

I remembered what he'd said to Troy after Meg lost it yesterday: *"Imagine what your life would be like if you had married her."* Yeah, sympathy wasn't going to work on Gooden. "Then maybe you could offer him some money for the ring?"

"You want me to bribe the sheriff? Have you lost your mind?"

Maybe. "Well, there has to be some way to get Granny O's ring out of evidence and onto your finger."

"Daryl Anne Blessing, I am not going to rob the evidence room."

"Of course not." That'd be crazy. Wouldn't it? Lord, what was I thinking? Gram would have another heart attack if I got myself arrested, especially inside the police station in the act of committing a felony. But I had to do something, and the only resolution that came to mind was bumping up my investigation—which also had the potential of landing me in handcuffs. And not the kind in those *Shades of Grey* books.

* * *

Between scheduled appointments and drop-in shoppers, the next two days hummed like a beehive. Constant mayhem. Happy brides, disappointed brides, frustrated brides, undecided brides, tearful brides. The whole gamut. The side of my brain that thrives on order had come close to imploding. I hadn't even thought about the Weddingville thief or come up with a sleuthing plan.

Right now, though, I was grateful for the lull this morning. I stood in the salon, finishing a cup of coffee, glancing out the window. Even foot traffic was thinner than it had been all week. It usually was on hump day. My gaze landed on Something Old, Something New across the street, and I stilled as if by an invisible hand. I hadn't been inside that shop since Bernice accused

Whitey of stealing the Roosevelt wedding server set. Irritation threatened to invade my moment of peace, and I stifled it. I'd rather focus on what was important. On finding the real thief. As I puzzled out how to do that, it occurred to me that I should start with the first robbery, start at the beginning. *Isn't that what Jessica Fletcher always does?*

Something tickled my neck, and I inhaled a whiff of sandalwood amid the heavier scent of the four bouquets of yellow roses. Mom had purchased them the other day from the Flower Girl and arranged the blooms throughout this room. I spun around to find Seth grinning, holding a single-stemmed orange rose toward me. He was like a spotlight targeting an actor on stage, his attention shining on me, filling me with warmth and vanquishing my shadowy thoughts. The smile in my heart sprang to my lips. I tilted my head and gazed into his twinkling brown eyes.

"An orange rose? Didn't you hear, Quinlan? The yellow ones were the better bargain."

He lifted a brow, leaning toward me with mischief in his dark eyes. In a low, husky voice, he said, "Yeah, but orange signifies fascination and desire, Blessing, and that's how I feel about you. Fascinated. And wanting you so much I can't even think."

He pulled me close, his mouth possessing mine in a mind-bending kiss. My stress fell away like snow melting from a roof as hot images of this man unleashed a need in me that left my knees weak and my brain addled. When we came up for air, I murmured, "Whew, you really know how to take a woman's mind off what's bothering her."

"Is something bothering you, Blessing?"

I hadn't had time to tell him about Meg and my visit to the O'Malleys the other day, but thinking about it now, I sighed. "Troy and Meg."

"How come?"

I leaned my head into his chest, his heart a steady thrumming in my ear as I brought him up to speed. "Joe swore to us that there was never a curse on that ring, and I think Meg actually accepted his word for it. But almost as soon as we left, she finally remembered what Granny O said about it."

"That the ring *is* cursed?" There was a touch of dread in his voice.

"I don't know if I'd call it a curse, more of a long-held sentiment." I explained what Meg recalled. "And Meg believes it with all her heart."

"It's a pretty romantic notion, but I don't see a problem. The ring has been found. You should be relieved, not worried. And Meg should be thrilled."

I peered up at him. "Not if the ring sits in some police evidence locker forever."

He frowned, digesting this for a long moment; then he held me gently by the shoulders, putting enough space between us to better see me. "But that means…"

I nodded. "That Meg and Troy are doomed unless the thief is caught and prosecuted right away."

"Honey, the police are working on that."

I rolled my eyes. "Considering the stellar investigative skills Gooden showed solving the murder of Meg's mother, how soon do you think he's likely to figure out who's ripping off Weddingville businesses?"

Seth pursed his lips. I knew he wanted to defend the sheriff's and Troy's abilities to clear this case, but he couldn't deny the chances were pretty slim. The thief could be anyone, from a town resident to someone passing through. "There must be another way to get the ring released from evidence."

"If you can make that happen, Meg and Troy would be forever grateful. Not to mention me." And I'd have a good time showing him exactly how thankful. "Can you?"

He offered up the same possibilities I'd come up with and finally gave up. "No. Short of solving the crime ourselves, I got nothing."

"I'm willing if you're willing."

He pulled me close again, kissing me long and sweet, and then, breathless, he stared at me like he was about to do what he'd done to me the night before. "I'm always willing where you're concerned, Blessing."

And I could feel the proof pressing my thigh. My own body screamed a responding, *Hell yes!* But the bridal shop salon was not the place, and this was not the time. I shoved my palm against his chest. "I meant, if you're willing to help me catch the thief."

"You? Us?" He released me like a match that had burned his fingertips.

I blinked. I'd just discovered how to deflate *the moment* in two easy seconds.

His raised eyebrows lowered, and he leaned toward me, looking as if I'd lost my mind. "Us?"

My mouth dried as I scrambled for a defense. "Yes. You and me. We could, um, investigate on our own. A little."

"Correct me if I'm wrong, Daryl Anne, but didn't Troy warn you not to get involved in an official police case?"

I could feel the heat spreading through my cheeks, and I started talking with the speed of an auctioneer. "Well, as a matter of fact he did, but see, this wouldn't be interfering exactly. It would just be us asking some questions of other shop owners or staff and putting fresh eyes on each of the robberies. We might come up with an angle the police haven't considered or maybe missed."

He shook his head and glanced toward the ceiling. "Lord, what have I gotten myself into falling for this woman?"

Did that mean he wasn't going to help? He grew thoughtful. He had to be weighing several things. The possibility of losing his part-time job with the police department if we were caught. His friendship with Troy. His wish for Troy to have a happy marriage. His natural inclination to rescue women in distress.

I waited. Patience, as you know by now, is not my strong suit, but I managed somehow to keep my yap shut while he processed my request. My phone vibrated. I checked the screen. A text from Meg: *Can you meet me at Zelda's right away?*

I responded, *What's up?*

Meg answered, *Something is missing from the shop. She swears it was there after the jewelry incident. And she doesn't want to call and report it to the police unless she has to. I'll explain why when you get here.*

I responded, *Okay, be right there.*

Gram strode in with a watering can. I told her and Seth, "I have to go out for a while. Can you cover for me, Billie?"

"Sure. Run along. If things get hectic, I'll text."

Before Seth could stop me or ask any questions, I said, "We'll talk later, okay?"

"Yes. We will."

The cryptic tone wasn't lost on me. It had been a long shot asking for his help, but maybe I wouldn't need it now.

Chapter 14

By the time I reached the wedding planner's shop, I was in full-on detecting mode, my mind rolling ideas faster than balls in a bingo cage. Zelda claimed the missing item had been in the shop *after* the jewelry was returned, but that didn't mean the thief hadn't come back again and taken whatever it was. Did it? I supposed that would depend on whatever was taken. Obviously, I needed more information.

I entered the shop with my senses heightened, especially my audio acuity. I hadn't noticed before but the door moved quietly on its hinges—no creak, no squeak, no cracking or popping like a lot of hundred-year-old buildings. Even more interesting was the lack of a bell or buzzer to signal customers coming in or leaving. In other words, it would be easy to sneak in and out without being noticed, especially if Zelda was busy. I wasn't sure what, if any, role that played in the thief dropping the stolen jewelry here, but it was a detail worth noting.

I started to call out, then stopped when I heard a murmur of voices nearby. Peering into the reception area, I spied three women—the wedding planner and two clients—seated around a small circular table.

My gaze, like that of a small child's, went straight to the brightest thing in the room. Zelda. Today's look brought to mind a fruity cocktail, yellow hair, and a lime and peach blouse over a strawberry skirt. On anyone else, it would be gaudy. On her, it worked. The other two women, a twentysomething and her mother, wore varying items of faded denim with splashes of red and white. Patriotic farm girls with unfortunate overbites.

I knew these two. The Hewitt/Barackman wedding. We'd ordered Ms. Barackman's gown, an old-fashioned lace, sans train, to accommodate her cowgirl boots. I remembered being told the theme was country chic, the reception being held in a barn that had been converted into a special events rental hall. The menu was barbeque and roasted pig.

Zelda seemed to be finalizing details for the shindig with them. She had set out props to show what she had in mind for decorations—a wagon wheel, a bale of hay, a pitchfork, and a cowboy hat. *To each his own,* I thought, suppressing a "yeehaw."

I nodded to them in recognition but didn't interrupt. Meg's stepmom was deep into her sales pitch. Ten Mason jar mugs and a giant glass bowl sat on the small table. "I bought this punch bowl set years ago," Zelda said, "and put them in a cupboard, waiting for the right bride and groom to come along. And here you are. I think this is perfect for your venue, Ms. Barackman."

Mother and daughter each picked up a mug, nodding. I wasn't sure which one of them said, "Perfect." Or, "Oh yes." It didn't matter.

"Oh good." Zelda put the punch bowl set back into its box, then placed a chocolate fountain on the table. "Do you think you'll want one of these?"

I left them to it, slipping into the next room where Meg had shown us the crimson slippers. But I wasn't thinking about wedding shoes. I was heading to the door marked PRIVATE, but I paused beside the bathroom. Could I believe the rumors about the jewelry being found in there?

My palms felt damp, my pulse jumpy. I peeked into the bathroom. I wasn't sure what I'd expected to find. Undetected clues poking from behind the commode? Fingerprint dust on every surface? A sign that said THE JEWELRY WAS LEFT HERE with an X to mark the spot? I sighed, disappointed and more than a little surprised at how white on white and sparkling clean the compact space was. No clues, no fingerprints, and no X.

My stomach dipped. Investigating looked easy on TV, but in real life, it was hard. Then again, I didn't have a script to work from or a prop department to stage the crime scene. If only I could see how this room looked prior to it being disinfected. Ah, but maybe I could. Seth had photos.

Yeah, like he's going to show you those. Maybe sleuthing meant covert spying. Maybe I was a bad girlfriend.

My gaze went to the toilet tank. Was that where the thief left the jewels? Nah. Zelda wouldn't have had any reason to look in there unless the works weren't working. Unless the jewels caused it not to flush. The mirror wasn't the kind with a medicine cabinet, rather one set in a filigree frame. There was a cupboard beneath the bowl sink, but it only contained a couple of rolls of TP, cleanser, and deodorizer. I checked behind the base of the toilet, then got to my feet, my gaze going back to the lid. Maybe I should check the tank just in case the cops missed something. Jessica Fletcher would do that. Right?

I reached for it with both hands.

"What're you doing?" Meg asked.

I jumped three feet, my heart landing in my throat. "Don't do that."

"I didn't mean to scare you. What's wrong? Is it running or something?"

"No. No." My cheeks heated with the guilt of a child being caught doing something I shouldn't. "I'm sure it's fine."

She frowned. "Daryl Anne, what's going on?"

I shrugged, pressing my lips flat. I needed to fess up. "I was just, you know, wondering about where the jewelry was found."

Meg made a face. "Not in the toilet tank."

"Do you know where?"

Zelda bustled in from the reception area.

"Oh, thank God, you're both here to help me look. I thought for a while there I'd lost my mind." Her plaintive voice echoed through the small shop. She waved a white sheet of paper like a surrender flag. "But see? The invoice. Those invitations are here somewhere."

I took it that the Barackmans had finished and departed. "Whose invitations are missing?"

Meg grabbed the invoice from Zelda's hand and read it, biting her bottom lip as she looked bug-eyed at me. "You won't believe it. It's Dillon and Willa Bridezilla's."

My eyes rounded. "Oh my God."

Zelda gazed from one of us to the other, worry in her voice. "Bridezilla? What do you two know that I don't?"

Meg and I exchanged wary glances that asked the silent question, *Should we tell her?*

I decided she had to know. "It's just that Willa can be a little demanding."

"Well, I've noticed she is a bit particular," Zelda said.

"Selfish," Meg said, sneering.

"High maintenance," I said as a counterpoint. Okay, let's face it. I was sugarcoating it.

"Well, her father likes to spoil her," Zelda said.

"Fiancé-stealing. Bitch. On. Wheels," Meg said.

"Oh, dear me. And she's due here any minute to pick up the invitations." Zelda seemed on the verge of hysteria.

Considering the meltdown she'd had the other day when the jewelry was found in her shop, God knew what this might bring on. I strove to keep her focused. "When is the wedding?"

I hoped the date allowed Zelda the time to reorder the invitations and spare her the wrath of Willa Bridezilla.

Zelda gave a shudder. "Three months. Plenty of time, but if she reacts as the two of you've suggested…"

"Oh, don't mind us. We were just teasing." Meg gave her stepmother a hug. Then she studied the invoice and read out loud, "The box contains two hundred wedding invitations."

"About what size would the box be?"

Zelda rattled off dimensions, making hand gestures for emphasis and then pointing to a small stack of boxes in the corner. "Like those."

I assumed she'd already checked each of those cartons, but fresh eyes sometimes found what panicky ones couldn't. Meg and I went through them again, reading the labels, lifting the lids and checking to be sure the customer name on the outer packaging matched the names on the invitations. The search proved fruitless, but we weren't giving up.

"When did you take possession of the now-missing invitations?" Maybe recalling the day the invitations arrived at the shop would jog her memory.

She considered, then said, "The same day I found the jewelry in the bathroom."

"Same time of day?"

"No. Around noon. I didn't find the jewelry until much later."

Zelda moaned. "Why can't I recall what I did after signing for the shipment?"

"Where else might you have put that box?" Meg asked.

Zelda wrung her hands, panic sweeping through her eyes. "In the storeroom or the cupboard, but I've already checked there."

Just the same, Meg and I double-checked both places, as well as everywhere Zelda suggested and some areas she didn't. Willa Bridezilla's box of invitations was nowhere in the little shop. Not in Zelda's car either. There was only one conclusion.

"Why would anybody steal a box of printed invitations?" Zelda said, sinking into a chair, a stunned expression clouding her usually sunny face. "It doesn't make sense."

I didn't get it either. "It's not like they could use them at their own wedding."

Meg smirked. "Unless their names are Dillon and Willa."

"Are you going to call the police?" I asked the question that had to also be running through both of their minds.

"Absolutely not," Zelda cried, getting to her feet. "But I am going to call Whitey about getting a couple of security cameras installed. Why didn't I take him up on that last week?"

Her words sent an unexpected chill through me.

* * *

The hot afternoon sun did nothing to eliminate the chill inside me. This was the second or third time that someone had hired Mom's boyfriend to install a security system *after* being robbed. Was Whitey robbing stores to drum up business?

"You still thinking about Willa?" Meg asked in a lowered voice as we settled at a table in Pre-Wedding Jitters, our favorite espresso drinks in hand.

I shot a sideways glance at Lisa Marie. She was busy waiting on a customer, the hissing of the espresso machine probably drowning Meg's question. Just the same, I was disinclined to pursue a conversation within the barista's earshot, about the woman who'd stolen her fiancé. I didn't want to talk about what was bothering me either. "No. Not her."

Meg narrowed her gaze, studying my readable face. "Then what has you looking like you're about to lose your best friend? Oh my God, you're not dumping me as your best friend, are you? I mean I know I've been a pain lately, but—"

"No. Absolutely not. Never." I couldn't believe she'd think such a thing, and I was pretty sure she could see that in my expression. I busied myself poking a straw into the lid of my drink—like that would make my suspicions about Whitey disappear. I'd considered sharing my secret worry with Seth, but his connection with the police had held me back, and what if I was wrong? What if my mother's boyfriend was innocent, and I put him on Sheriff Gooden's radar? I needed Meg to talk me off this wall. I had to confide in her. She always kept my secrets. Only this time I'd be asking her to keep something related to a police case from Troy. I jammed my hand through my hair, choking back a feral scream.

Meg grasped my hand. "Seriously, Daryl Anne, if you won't talk, you'll force me to guess."

I sighed. "It was what Zelda said about having Whitey install a security system in her shop."

"And...?"

"And, this is like the second or third time a Weddingville merchant has decided to hire his services *after* being ripped off."

Meg gasped, making the leap without my filling in the gap. "You think Whitey is the thief?"

"Shhh. Someone will hear you."

"Sorry." Meg's eyes were huge as she leaned across the table, her voice a whisper. "Oh, your poor mom."

"Then you don't think I'm wrong or that it could just be coincidental?" I really, really wanted her to tell me that I was jumping to conclusions.

"Yeah, if it had happened once. Or even twice. But three times?"

I groaned.

A dawning look filled her eyes. "Oh, that's why you were looking so distraught. Your mom. You were wise not to go straight back to the bridal shop. She would've taken one look at you and you would've caved in less than twenty questions. You're not a good liar, Daryl Anne."

"I don't want to lie. I just want to be wrong. This is the first guy she's dated in all these years."

Meg bit her bottom lip. "Maybe Troy could—"

"No. You have to promise that you won't say a word to anyone, especially Troy, unless we can find proof."

"Proof? What are we going to do, break into his house or place of business?"

"Maybe." I hadn't thought that far ahead, but it wasn't like it would be the first time the two of us had bent the law for a good cause. Or searched a suspect's abode. "Maybe there's something in his van that would tell us what we want to know."

"Have you forgotten that you're talking about a security expert? His home, office, and van will all be impenetrable by the likes of us."

Oh sure. Throw facts at me. "God, you're right. Maybe we could follow him around."

"For what reason? To catch him in the act?"

"To see if the next person he approaches ends up burglarized."

The door of the coffee shop opened, and Meg visually cringed. "Don't look now, but it's the Gossip Sisters."

I didn't have to look. They sneaked up behind me before I could turn around. Velda's voice hit my ears like a nail file on metal. "What are you two conspiring about on this lovely summer afternoon?"

"Yeah," Jeanette said. "We figured you'd be at work, like Wanda."

They'd figured? Why were Meg and I even a topic of conversation between these women? Not wanting to encourage their curiosity, I kept my answer brief. "Slow day."

"Hot day, you mean," Velda said. "My throat's parched. Lisa Marie, I'll take one of your special iced coffees. Bigger the better."

"Ooh, wait for me, Velda," Jeanette said, scurrying to the counter. "Make mine a Creamy Strawberry Frappé with lots of whipped cream on top."

"Must be nice to never have to worry about your weight." Meg nodded toward the bony Jeanette.

"Or diabetes," I said, thinking of Gram and then realizing I really needed to get back to work. "We should go."

"What are you going to do about Whitey?" Meg asked.

"I'm not sure yet."

"Be careful. If he is doing this, he could be dangerous."

I hadn't considered that. It was bad enough that I even suspected him, but if he was capable of committing a crime to increase his business, what might he do to keep from being exposed? Was Mom in danger just dating Whitey? Maybe I should reconsider enlisting Seth's help. "I guess I need a foolproof plan."

"You need a poker face." Meg sipped her drink. "And now that the Gossip Sisters have their drinks, we should go."

We gathered our to-go cups as Lisa Marie set Jeanette's drink on the counter. The whipped cream was two inches high.

The door to the shop banged open. I jumped, nearly dropping my latte. I spun toward the new customer and froze, as stunned as if Elvis himself stood there. But it wasn't the ghost of the king of rock and roll. It was Willa Bridezilla. The tiny brunette's face was as red as the strawberries in Jeanette's Frappé.

She spied Lisa Marie and bristled. If I were casting a movie about the "other woman," I couldn't have chosen more perfectly. Lisa Marie was dressed in cutoff jeans, her long legs tan and lean, her tank top barely holding in her generous curves. Sexy barista.

Willa, on the other hand, wore white slacks and a navy silk T-shirt, heavy gold jewelry, and strappy espadrilles. Rich princess.

The air vibrated with tension, holding everyone in place as still and lifeless as the giant cardboard Elvis near the counter.

"You bitch!" Willa screamed, pointing at Lisa Marie. "You stole them, and I want them back now."

Lisa Marie went as stiff as the handle on the espresso machine. "I don't know what you're talking about. And for the record, I don't take what doesn't belong to me."

"Liar!" Willa shrieked. "Give me back my invitations or I'll have you arrested, bitch."

Lisa Marie shifted her head as if taking in and digesting the accusation. "Someone stole your wedding invitations?" She started to laugh and laugh. "Thank you, Karma."

"I want my invitations back. Now." Willa barreled toward the counter like a mini-steamroller without any care who might be in her path.

"You bat-shit crazy skank, get out of my shop."

I should've stayed out of it, but as much as I often resented Gram's Bunko buddies, I couldn't leave them in harm's way. I wasn't quick enough. Willa snatched Jeanette's Frappé, elbowing the poor woman aside, and hurled the drink at Lisa Marie. Bull's-eye. Strawberries and ice cubes slammed into the barista's head, turning her hair a bright pink as if she were bleeding from a scalp wound. Whipped cream slid down her nose to cling at its tip.

Jeanette didn't fare much better. She hit the wall and slid to the floor, her eyes glazed.

I was unable to stop my forward momentum. I bumped into Velda. She yelped, tossing her hands skyward. Her iced coffee launched straight toward the ceiling, seemed to hang there for a nanosecond, and then began to fall, the lid flipping free. *Splat.* Tan liquid spattered across Willa's white slacks. Somehow Velda and I ended up sprawled on the floor with the cardboard Elvis. The full skirt of my sundress absorbed the gooey, chilled coffee like a sponge, wetting my bottom. Velda mirrored the dazed sensation gripping me.

"Look at me! You're going to pay for this," Willa shouted, throwing a tantrum as if someone else, not her, had perpetrated this terrible mess. I wanted to smack her, but Lisa Marie beat me to it.

"Oh, shut up," she said, dumping a full pitcher of strawberries and juice on Willa's head. The juice ran across the floor, joining the iced coffee already soaking into my clothing.

"Auk!" Willa squealed. "I'm allergic to strawberries."

Lisa Marie chuckled. "You're lucky it wasn't gasoline."

"You all heard that." Willa indicated each of us; then her index finger shifted like the pointer on a compass dial to Lisa Marie. Hatred blazed in her eyes. "She threatened to kill me."

Chapter 15

The door to the coffee shop slammed as Willa stormed out.

"This is your fault, Daryl Anne," Velda said as I helped her to her feet.

I arched a brow. "How do you figure that?"

"If you'd have stayed where you were, I wouldn't have ended up on the floor, sopping wet."

"No good deed," I muttered, tugging the saturated seat of my skirt away from my body.

"You'd all better leave," Lisa Marie said. "I'm closing down for the day."

"But I need my iced coffee," Velda said, heaving herself to the counter. "I paid for it."

Lisa Marie plunked the money onto the counter. Velda shoved it back at her. "I don't want my money back. I want my iced coffee."

"And I didn't get my Frappé." Jeanette was fussing with her own damp maxi dress, wringing the hem like a soaked washcloth.

"I'm out of strawberries." Lisa Marie waved her hands, gesturing to the pink mess on pretty much every surface in the room and on a couple of us.

"Well, that's not Jeanette's fault," Velda said.

Lisa Marie slapped Jeanette's money down beside Velda's and then grabbed a rag from the sink and swiped at the whipped cream on her face, irritation tightening her jaw. "Go. Now. I need to deal with this mess."

She shooed us out the door like a bunch of yowling cats. Velda glared at me. "You're going to be sorry, Daryl Anne."

Translation: my mother and Billie are going to hear about it. And probably most of the town.

Meg's hands landed on her hips. "How do you figure that, Velda?"

Velda pointed at me. "She knows." With that, she grabbed Jeanette's arm and started off in the direction of the Wedding Cakery—likely to update Wanda on the excitement she'd missed, as well as bad-mouth me.

I was still puzzling how any of what had happened was my fault as Meg and I chose a different route to Front Street. The warm afternoon held a soft breeze that lifted the full skirt of my sundress, quickly drying the dampness from my backside. If only it could remove the stickiness.

Meg was lost in her own thoughts. Finally she said, "Do you think Lisa Marie might have taken the invitations?"

I considered the possibility. "You mean to ruin Willa and Dillon's wedding?"

Meg nodded.

"Nah. There's plenty of time to reorder invitations. And based on what we just observed, Lisa Marie doesn't strike me as one to go looking for trouble. Or even revenge."

"But she won't back down if trouble comes to her."

"Exactly. If she was into revenge, I think she's more the type who would show up at the ceremony with a paint ball gun."

Meg laughed, picking a strawberry from the hem of my dress. "Yeah, I could see that."

"Besides," I said on a sigh, "we know Lisa Marie isn't the Weddingville thief."

I just didn't know then that she was much worse.

* * *

Do you have any idea how hard it is to spy on someone whose living is made unmasking others' bad behavior? Someone with watchdog eyes and a security guard mentality? Neither did I. Until I tried it over the next two days.

Oh, I thought I'd considered all the angles, everything that might give me away. Including my face. But the one thing I hadn't calculated was how I'd react to what I was doing. I couldn't turn off my emotions like a switch. I couldn't disconnect from them like a cord in a wall socket. I couldn't keep my palms from getting damp, or my mouth from drying, or my stomach from pinching.

At first, it felt as if I were doing okay. Whitey didn't seem to notice the nervous hitch in my voice. A certain confidence started to seep through the nerves as I casually asked him who he'd pitched his security systems to in town. Simple enough. I took mental notes of all the stores he'd visited. Then I asked who, if any, of those proprietors had hired his services. Nothing suspicious about that question either. In fact, Whitey seemed more than willing to dish.

But in the back of my mind, I kept chewing on what it would do to Mom if I discovered he was the Weddingville thief and worrying that he might be a danger to her. She deserved a good guy. A great guy. Maybe Whitey was that guy, but what if he wasn't?

In the end, the worry proved my downfall.

Whitey didn't catch on. Seth did.

I felt his stare before I glanced in his direction. His narrowed brown eyes seemed darker than sable and gave me pause. I could tell he was trying to figure out what I was doing, what I was thinking. Well, he could keep wondering. No amount of monetary offering could pry it out of me. But then, he had other means of persuasion to which I wasn't immune.

Best to avoid him altogether. Of course, that proved impossible. He found me at the coffee machine. "Blessing, what are you up to?"

"Nothing." My glance shifted to the left in the classic way of all liars. "Much."

His sexy mouth lifted on one corner, and he shook his head. "Does your mother know you don't trust her boyfriend?"

Guilt shot through me, and denial spilled through my lips. "No. That's not true."

"Yeah, it is. But what I'm wondering is why? Did you find evidence that he's cheating on her?" He studied me for a long moment, then quirked his head. "Or do you suspect him of another kind of crime?"

"Shh," I said. "He's right behind you."

"Gearing up for another busy day?" Whitey asked, striding to the counter, coffee cup in one hand, his phone in the other.

"Yep," Seth answered, recovering his poise twice as fast as me. "You?"

Whitey set his empty cup in the sink. "I'm off to see Wanda Perroni this morning."

"Excuse me?" I needed to clean the wax from my ears. I couldn't have heard him correctly. "Did you say Wanda? Wedding Cakery Wanda?"

He grinned as if we shared a private joke. "She wants to put in some security cameras."

I didn't believe it. More likely she wanted to give Whitey "the scoop" about his girlfriend's daughter's antics at Pre-Wedding Jitters the other day. I heard suspicion in my voice. "Why?"

"Someone stole a cake from her bakery yesterday," he said.

My mouth dropped open. "Really? A cake? I could see a donut or even a few cookies, but how does someone sneak out a cake without being noticed?"

Whitey shrugged.

Seth said, "It was a wedding cake."

"A wedding cake? Impossible." I wasn't buying this.

"Not really," Whitey said. "When I was there the other day, I noticed a couple of gaps Wanda has in security."

When he was there the other day? He'd gone back a second time to try and sell Wanda a security system after the first debacle? That took balls. And determination. I wasn't sure if I respected him for that or thought him a fool. A little of both, I supposed. It also made him even more suspect since he'd seen a way to take something from the shop, and then someone had.

I shook my head. "I can't get over someone taking a wedding cake."

"It was a small one," Seth said.

"So you knew about this?" Actually the question was why no one had told me. Had I been kicked off the grapevine? Did Gram and Mom know? Surely Gram did. On the other hand, she'd been preoccupied the past two days after her checkup with the doctor. He was considering calling in a wrist specialist, which might mean another surgery. Mom and I had been trying to keep her spirits up, but I wasn't sure we were succeeding—because the idea worried us both too much.

"I heard the police investigated," Whitey said, pulling me back to the cake robbery. "Did they find any clues, Seth?"

"Nothing I can talk about," Seth said, staring pointedly at Whitey as if he were also thinking along the same lines as me.

Was he? Or was I coloring innuendoes to suit my investigative theories? What if I was wrong? What if Whitey's interest was nothing more than curiosity? I rubbed the nape of my neck, coming slowly to the conclusion that I needed a refresher course in Sleuthing 101.

"I gotta run. Have a great day," Whitey said, giving Mom a peck on the cheek as she came in. "See you later, Susan. Wish me luck."

"You're all the luck you need," Mom assured him. The love I saw in her eyes when she turned toward us was strictly for the man hurrying out the back door, and I felt something inside me shift. I had to find proof that Whitey was innocent, or my mother was going to take an emotional hit that could send her back into spinster mode for another fifteen years.

She snapped her fingers in an oh-I-forgot-to-tell-you gesture. "Daryl Anne, before I forget, I took the precaution of moving Meg's wedding dress into your bedroom closet. I'm probably worrying for nothing, but after her ring went missing, well, you know, I didn't want to risk that disappearing too."

"That poor girl," Gram said, coming in from alterations to accept the cup of coffee Seth had poured for her. "Even though we have the security system, I still don't know if we're much safer."

Seth's gaze met mine and conveyed the message that our conversation, although interrupted, was not done. "Ladies, I have a couple of photo shoots today. I'll be out most of the day. If anyone inquires about my services, I've left out brochures, business cards, and a sign-up sheet for anyone wanting to leave their name and number."

He squeezed my shoulder as he passed me, whispering softly, "Dinner tonight?"

He'd been so busy fulfilling existing bookings that we hadn't had another evening together. Or even much time. I answered his invitation with a warm smile as my heart clenched in anticipation. "You'd better bring your piggy bank if you plan on me spilling secrets, though."

I heard his soft chuckle long after he'd left the room.

"Did you hear about the theft at the Wedding Cakery?" I asked my parental units, still a bit upset that no one had told me.

"How does someone sneak a wedding cake out of a bakery?" Hannah asked as she emerged from alterations.

Mom, Gram, and I suggested possible scenarios, some of them absurd and hilarious, but Hannah remained her usual strange self. She hung in the shadows, making me think she could slip in and out of a space without anyone noticing her. Like wallpaper. Like a sneak thief. And then I felt her breath on my neck as she whispered, "These thefts are strange…like someone is stealing a wedding."

"Geesh, Hannah." I brushed the air as if I were swatting at a fly. How had she moved from across the room to behind me without me noticing? "Stop sneaking up on me."

"Sorry."

But I doubted she was. She just didn't seem to have developed any social skills.

"Oh, Daryl Anne, would you go to the Flower Girl for me this morning and pick up the roses for the shop? Flora is too busy to deliver them. Whitey said he'd fetch them when he goes to his appointment with her later, but I want the flowers before we open today. We have a full schedule of appointments."

"Flora's getting a security system?" Gram asked. "Don't tell me that she was robbed, too?"

"What?" Mom quirked her head. "Oh no, dear. She just decided to install a couple of cameras. Better safe than sorry, like some others in this town."

Meaning Bernice, I thought.

"Smart woman," Jenny said, coming in from the storeroom, wearing her usual black skirt and crisp white blouse. If I were casting her in a TV show, she'd be "young, no-nonsense, personal secretary." The only flaw was the missing button near her waist. I made a mental note to tell her.

Jenny smoothed a hand over her sleek ponytail. "Some of those antique planters and wall and garden accessories in the florist shop are expensive items. There's an ironwork trellis that I'd love to have for my garden wedding."

"Well, I say it's a shame," Billie said, "that everyone in this town feels the need to lock up and spy on every passerby. Give me the old days when no one locked their doors."

I was with Gram. I wanted to go back two weeks to when everyone felt safe, when neighbors didn't cast sidelong glances at one another.

* * *

It always feels like I'm walking into a secret garden when I enter a floral shop. Green everywhere. Take another step and bursts of color catch the eye. But the first sensation is the ambrosia scent, a mix of different blooms that I can never quite define. Sweet. Pleasant.

This was the Flower Girl. The narrow entrance, like walking through a trellis, opened to a wide room that held racks and displays and an array of accessories for garden and home, just as

Jenny had described. The mesh of voices, however, robbed the sense of a secret garden today.

Customers milled throughout the display racks, oohing and aahing at the variety of arrangements. Several were almost nose-touching the glass cooler case, peering in at myriad bouquets in a riot of hues that could suit any wedding theme.

As I worked my way toward the counter, I spied Flora working the cash register. Her daughter, Violet, and another person I didn't recognize were in the work area behind her, putting together arrangements.

Flora looked up, spotting me in line. She was in her late forties with thick glasses, straight blond hair going gray, and a penchant for oversized jeans and men's plaid shirts. She waved me forward, leaned across the counter, and said, "Daryl Anne, your mother's roses are in the cooler in the storeroom. Just go on back and get them."

"Sure." I retreated along the line of buyers waiting to pay for treasures they'd found or to place an order for that something special that would add to their own perfect ceremony. *At the end of the day,* I thought, *there are worse jobs than fulfilling someone's dreams.* I cut across the room to a doorway marked EMPLOYEES ONLY, humming "Here Comes the Bride."

I entered a short hallway that opened into a ten-by-twenty-foot windowless room. I suppressed a shudder, telling myself it wasn't some creepy basement, just a storeroom. But the sputtering fluorescent lighting overhead did not alleviate my unease. I hummed a little louder. My gaze darted to the shelves at one end of the room, stuffed with boxes, vases, planters, and big plastic buckets. Nothing there to cause the hair on my nape to stand on end. And yet it was.

My arms were even goose bumpy. *Stop it, Daryl Anne.* All the talk about locking doors and no one feeling safe in this town had me scaring up nightmares in the daytime. *Nothing scary, except maybe a spider or two.* My gaze went to the two refrigeration units at the other end of the room. The glass front of the larger cooler seemed frosted, but as I neared, I realized it was just steamed up, as if someone had let too much warm air into the interior by holding the door open too long.

I peered into the smaller cooler first. Baby's breath, lilies, carnations, even lilacs, but no roses. I moved to the other cooler, grabbed the handle, and pulled the door open. Chilled air rushed out to greet me. I stared at the calamity inside, not comprehending what I was seeing. It looked as if someone had taken a baseball bat to the glass shelving, vases, and flowers, smashing everything. Shards of glass clattered to the concrete, onto my sandal-clad feet, cutting into my toes.

I didn't feel it. Not then. My attention zeroed in on the mound of rose petals and broken stems on the bottom of the cooler. A fisted hand rose from the heap as if reaching toward me. I recoiled. I wanted to run. But what if this person was alive? Needing help. I leaned forward to touch the wrist and felt cold, rubbery flesh. Someone started screaming. It might've been me.

Chapter 16

I lost time and my breakfast, contaminating the crime scene. At some point, I became aware of someone speaking to me, and as my vision began to focus and the numbness receded from my brain, I found myself staring at Troy's handsome face and wondering what he was doing here.

Worry radiated from his bright blue eyes. "Daryl Anne, can you hear me? You've had a little shock."

A little shock? More like a seismic jolt, I realized as memories awoke, swarming me like a hive of angry bees. I struggled to sit up. I was seated on a hard bench set against a wall. I glanced around. I was still in the storeroom but no longer alone. Three or four official-looking people in uniforms were gathered around the coolers. I could hear one voice mumbling orders.

I began to shake. "W-who is it?"

Sheriff Gooden came into my line of vision. "Deputy O'Malley, there will be no leaking of information. Need to know only. Identity has to be confirmed, family notified."

"But I found the body," I said with authority, forgetting I had none. To my currently shaky reasoning, finding the body meant that I had a right to know a few things. Like who it was. And how they'd died. And probably who'd killed them. I glanced toward the ceiling, instinctively looking for a camera, then remembered that Whitey was going to be meeting with Flora today about installing surveillance devices. So no camera footage of the murder.

Murder. I shuddered, my gag reflex kicking in. Troy jammed a plastic bucket in front of me. When I looked up, I saw the sheriff rubbing his jaw like a man thinking of early retirement. Two murders in three months was more than he'd signed on for. He hadn't exactly done himself proud solving the last one, and if he couldn't do better with this one, the body in the cooler wouldn't be the only thing dead.

I couldn't, however, fault him on procedure. "We'll need a statement, Daryl Anne, and to print you."

"Print me?" I gaped, my mouth drying. Was he trying to pin this on me? I supposed that would be the easiest resolution for his shoot-the-messenger mentality and his desperation to salvage his career. A new round of shivers wracked through me. I tried to stop my knees from knocking and failed. "Do I need a lawyer?"

"No," Troy said. "The fingerprinting is to distinguish yours from all the others that might be on the cooler, in order to eliminate you as a suspect."

Eliminate me? That means I'm a person of interest.

"I touched the handle," I said. And the corpse's wrist—that cold, cold wrist. Could fingerprints be extracted from skin? I gagged again. Fortunately, there was nothing more left in my stomach to expel.

The sheriff eyed me like a third-time offender he couldn't wait to send to the big house. His hand reached for his utility belt, hovering near a set of handcuffs. I cringed. "You can't arrest me. I don't even know who died."

Apparently the hysterical edge in my voice was reason for concern and quick action. Troy and Gooden said in unison, "No one's arresting you, Daryl Anne."

Then Seth came through the doorway, and I swear I heard angels sing and saw light form a halo around his tawny hair. Then again, maybe it was the shock. A camera hung at his hip and one around his neck. The normalcy of that comforted me. I wanted to run to him, to wrap myself in his arms until I felt normal again. But I didn't think I could get to my feet. Besides, he wasn't here for me. He'd been called away from his appointment to photograph this crime scene. I cringed. I didn't want him to see what I'd seen. Or worse. Even if it was his job.

He didn't see me. He headed toward the cooler, greeting someone there with a solemn response. Whoever it was must've immediately mentioned my being there because he spun in my direction, worry shaping his mouth into an O. Our gazes collided, mine growing wide as the person I couldn't see told him I'd found the body.

Sheriff Gooden ordered him to stay clear of me. Seth ignored the order and rushed to my side. "Blessing," he said, gathering me in his arms, my knight in shining armor.

Oh God, he feels solid and warm and safe. I stifled a sob but couldn't contain the next one, or the next. I cried until the front of his shirt was damp, until the impulse calmed. He held me tight the whole while, never wavering, just comforting me. Apparently my outburst had subdued the others as well, including the sheriff.

When I finally felt in control again, I eased from Seth's embrace, embarrassed that I'd fallen apart in front of an audience. But I didn't apologize. Except to Seth. He used his clean hankie to dry my damp face, holding my cheek in one hand as he spoke. "I'd take you back to the bridal shop, but I'm needed here right now."

I nodded.

"I'll see she gets home," Troy said. "I've called Meg. She'll meet you there."

Turned out, it would take more than my BFF to soothe what ailed me.

* * *

I was certain it must be afternoon by now, but as Troy and I entered the bridal shop through the back door, we found Gram, Jenny, and Hannah still in the coffee area, chatting instead of waiting on customers. The wall clock showed ten minutes to opening.

Billie glanced at me, eyebrows lifting. "Daryl Anne, you don't have the roses. Didn't Flora have our order ready?"

I shook my head, afraid that I'd fall apart again if I tried to explain.

"Personally," Hannah said, "I can't stand the smell of roses."

"Oh, I love that fragrance." Jenny blew on the steaming mug she held, her crisp black and white look contrasting with Hannah's careless appearance. "Reminds me of Brad's mother's garden."

"Or a funeral home," Hannah mumbled.

"Don't say such things, Hannah," Gram admonished. "It's liable to give the grim reaper ideas. I came too close to making his acquaintance a couple months ago. I don't need a repeat."

"I doubt he's listening to me, Billie," Hannah retorted, her tone full of cynicism.

"Especially in this place where happiness is on sale every day," Jenny said.

"Yeah, we're a regular Disneyland of the bridal world," Hannah mumbled, eyeing Jenny like she would a bouquet of wilted roses.

I stifled the urge to scream at Hannah that someone had died violently a few doors down, and she was here, alive, breathing, with a chance for happiness. If only she'd try. But she wasn't going to change. *What is it they say about relatives? You can't choose them?* I rubbed the nape of my neck, curbing my irritation. Hannah was too easy of a target. In my current mood, I might say something I couldn't take back or that I'd regret later when I wasn't trembling like a wet cat.

Hannah leveled her dull gaze on me, but whatever she'd been about to say was lost as she took a long look at me. I'd been crying. I was pretty sure my nose rivaled Rudolph's on Christmas Eve. She took an involuntary step toward me, her hand reaching out. "Daryl Anne...what's happened?"

The sincere caring touched my heart arousing such emotion that words choked in my throat.

"There's been a death at the Flower Girl," Troy said, stepping forward. "Daryl Anne found the body."

A collective gasp issued from the three women. Gram went pale, but color rushed into Hannah's normally pale cheeks, her eyes losing their half-mast dullness to a wide-awake stare.

"How awful for you," Jenny said.

But it was Hannah who came to help me, leading me to a bar stool, making sure I sat.

Isn't it strange how something totally obtuse crosses your mind in the wake of a jarring shock? This was the first time I'd seen my cousin blush in recent years. The animation transformed her. As everyone reacted to the news, I pondered the change in Hannah. *She's actually lovely,* I realized. *Pretty, even.* Her beauty was usually hidden by an apathetic nature, as though she were hiding from the world, discouraging anyone from noticing her. When had that happened, and why hadn't I noticed before today?

As everyone fussed over me, I struggled to recall what kind of child Hannah had been. *Spirited* came to mind. I know I said she was a sneaky, sticky-fingered kid, but was that a fair assessment? Had I been remembering right? Or not? I couldn't be sure.

Mostly I remembered what a pest she was, always into my stuff, always wanting to tag along with me and Meg. But then to a teenager, any child is a pain when they're five years younger. She'd probably only wanted to be included back then. And now she seemed to want to be excluded. What had caused such a dramatic shift? I made a mental note to find out. *Sleuthing isn't limited to murder and jewelry heists.*

"Was it Violet?" Hannah asked me, fear taking over her initial shock, her voice shaky.

"I don't know." I glanced at Troy. "Was it?"

He wore his cop mask, remaining silent for several seconds. I didn't think he was going to tell us, and I knew I'd hate him for letting us speculate and worry for hours on end. But he had a good heart. He sighed. "It wasn't Violet."

"Then who was it?" Gram's voice brooked no nonsense. That need-to-know gene obviously ran in the family.

Troy's palm shot up like a stop sign at a school crossing. "I can't give out a name until identification has been confirmed and family notified. Please. Don't keep asking."

Gram ignored his edict and pulled out the I-used-to-change-your-diapers card. "At least tell us if it's someone we know, Troy O'Malley."

"Billie, I'm not allowed to divulge that information." Troy sounded stern, but a line of red along his jaw gave away his discomfiture. "Daryl Anne, are you going to be okay? Meg should be here any minute. I have to get back to…" He walked toward the door as he spoke, leaving his last statement unfinished as he hurried out.

Gram grumbled, "No reason we shouldn't be told who died."

"Daryl Anne found the body," Jenny said, as if being reminded wouldn't upset me more. She brought to mind a voyeur at a fatal accident, craning her neck for a better view, for a glimpse of the blood and gore. "She knows who it is, don't you, Daryl Anne?"

"D-do you?" Hannah asked softly, almost cringing from the idea.

"No…he…she"—surely that hand poking from the heap of flowers was too small to belong to a man—"the face was covered with rose petals."

Someone gasped. Maybe Hannah. Gram had her hand to her mouth.

Jenny leaned toward me, her ponytail swishing. "Didn't you move them and, you know, peek?"

"No."

"Of course you didn't." Hannah recoiled, as did I, at the very thought.

Jenny's hands went to her hips. "Well, I only meant that she might've brushed the petals aside while checking to see if the person was still alive."

"No. Whoever it was, was not alive." The feel of that cold flesh returned, and I thought my knees might collapse.

"That settles it," Gram intervened, cutting Jenny off before she could ask more gruesome questions. I breathed a sigh of relief. Gram said, "We're closing for the day."

"But I have two brides coming for final fittings," Hannah said.

"When they arrive, you and I can see to them," Gram assured

her. "But no one's getting in today without an appointment. Jenny, you can help me put the sign in the window letting customers know that we're doing appointments only. Then you can have the rest of the day off."

Jenny pouted, as if she were being punished instead of getting a paid afternoon to spend anyway she liked. "All right. Maybe Lisa Marie will know who's dead. She hears all the news."

I shuddered again, eyeing Hannah. She said, "Would you like some coffee? Or maybe a whisky? I've heard that's good for shock."

"No. Thank you, though," I said, offering her a grateful smile.

The rest of the day was a blur. Mom arrived, then swept me into the elevator and up to the third-floor apartment we shared with Gram. Meg and I had no time alone with Mom hovering. She fussed over me like a five-year-old with a bad fever. She insisted I take a hot bath, have some herbal tea and toast, and climb into bed. I didn't think I'd sleep, but I zonked. I suffered a couple of bad dreams, but nothing major. I woke to discover I'd slept the afternoon away.

Mom began to hover again. While I appreciated her concern, a grown woman can only take so much coddling from her mother. So when Seth showed up, suggesting he'd like to take me to his house and fix me dinner and dessert, I jumped at the invitation. Dessert turned out to be my favorite—hot naked male who couldn't get enough of me. Kisses sweeter than ripe cherries, touches more fiery than flambé, and pleasure as decadent as the richest chocolate.

We fell asleep entwined, my sense of security returned. No nightmares invaded my dreams, and I didn't wake until daylight peeked through the blinds and Sonny whined to go outside. Seth was still dozing as I eased out of his arms and slipped from the bed, to discover I was sore in a few new places, but otherwise, fully restored to my pre-finding-a-corpse-in-a-cooler-self.

As I started the coffeepot, I let Sonny out the back door and filled his dish with food and water. By the time I'd showered and dressed, I was determined to get some answers. I texted Meg to meet me out front of Cold Feet Café. She agreed. I brought Sonny in and left Seth a note; then I slipped outside into the early morning air, tugging up the zipper of my sweatshirt hoodie as I hurried along the sidewalk toward the diner.

The sky was a glorious blue, the air rife with a briny twinge and the odor of frying bacon. Traffic, both street and sidewalk, was slight. Usually, temperatures are a bit cooler near the water, but today the air felt several degrees warmer than earlier in the week. I suspected the afternoon and evening would be one of those picnic nights where families gather outdoors to share homemade dishes, play games with their kids, and catch up on each others' lives.

I spotted Meg as I neared the diner, and she spotted me. She started walking toward me, studying me like a psychiatrist looking for tics in a mental patient. It was as if we'd reversed roles. I was usually worrying over her state of mind, but now she was the one obviously fretting over mine. How I longed for the normalcy we'd had before returning to Weddingville. If, that is, one could call living and working in the entertainment industry normal.

Meg seemed subdued, her unruly curls pulled into a thick braid, her makeup subtle, her eyes clear. Even her attitude struck me as different. There was a confidence in her step that had been missing since before she'd almost married Peter. My BFF was finally reemerging. My heart did a happy flip.

She smiled and gave me a quick hug. "Are you okay?"

"Turns out I'm pretty tough," I reassured her, a quality we shared this day. "Do you know anything new?"

She shook her head. "Troy won't tell me a danged thing."

"I figured. But I've been mulling over something that Jenny said yesterday, and I think it's worth exploring. If it doesn't pay off, we can console ourselves with a great latte."

We headed back toward Blessing's Bridal, Meg on the shop side of the sidewalk so that I wouldn't have to face the Flower Girl. Her plan to protect me went awry when Flora came bustling out, waving at us. "Yoohoo, Meg, Daryl Anne, wait up."

Of course the first thing I wondered was how the florist was dealing with having a dead body stuffed into her flower cooler. She seemed a little flustered, her plaid shirt buttoned unevenly, her glasses smeared, running one sentence into another, making little or no sense. Meg and I nodded and inserted "yes" and "no" where it seemed appropriate. And then I began to wonder if maybe she knew who'd been in her cooler.

"No," she said. "Sheriff Gooden had just come into the shop when you started screaming. He shooed me out along with all of my customers."

One of whom could well have been the killer, I thought, surprised that the sheriff had taken that action. *Stellar police work, Gooden.*

"I'm so very sorry, Daryl Anne, for what you went through."

Probably better me than Flora, I thought, realizing how distraught she was. "I'm sorry, too, but it's not your fault."

But whose fault was it? That was the question. The problem in solving this crime, however, was that I didn't know who'd been killed. So how was I supposed to come up with a motive?

Meg caught my arm. "We have to go."

"Oh, sure." Flora pushed her glasses higher on her nose. "But, oh, wait, the reason I stopped you. I almost forgot. I've tried to reach Troy, Meg, but he's not answering his phone. Could you give him a message for me? He wanted to know if I was missing anything, what with all the thefts in town. I told him I wasn't, but then I wasn't thinking very clearly, was I? It wasn't until this morning that I discovered it's gone."

"What's gone?" My attention snapped to Flora.

"The bouquet I finished shortly before you came in, Daryl Anne. It was in the cooler that wasn't destroyed. It's not there now."

Hannah's eerie words zinged through my mind: *It's like someone's stealing a wedding.*

"It was actually a sample bouquet. The customer wanted to take it home and think it over."

"Who was the customer?" Meg asked.

"What, oh, ah, what is her name? She reminds me of an Echinopsis blooming cactus, lovely to look at and just as prickly. Darn, why can't I recall her name?" Flora frowned, then brightened. "Trillum. No, that's not it, but something close to that."

"Willa—" I broke off before I added Bridezilla.

"Oh, yes, that's it, Willa, er, something. Sorry. I can't seem to remember anything today."

Meg's gaze met mine, and she seemed to be adding up awful possibilities as quickly as I was.

I said, "We do have to go, Flora. Right now."

Meg nodded. "I'll see that Troy knows about this, Flora, as soon as I see him. Thank you for telling us."

We set off, both lost in thought. When we were beyond Flora's hearing, Meg said, "Do you suppose the body in the cooler was Willa Bridezilla?"

I recalled the small, cold hand fisted as if clenching something. A bad feeling settled in my stomach. "Maybe."

We picked up our pace. Meg must have sensed the same unease that was plaguing my every step. The urge to hurry to Pre-Wedding Jitters before it was too late. But too late for what? Half a block away, I had the answer. I glanced at Meg, dread filling me. "We're too late."

Police cars, lights flashing, were angled at the door to the coffee shop. As we watched, moving closer and closer, we spied Troy and Sheriff Gooden escorting Lisa Marie, her hands cuffed behind her back, to one of the patrol sedans.

"Oh no. Does this mean it *was* Willa Bridezilla?" Meg asked as we kept moving toward the chaos.

"It sure seems like it." Why else would the police arrest our favorite barista?

"How awful." Meg all but whispered the words, her tone suggesting she'd had another reminder of just how quickly things one takes for granted can change—not always for the better.

I didn't speak. I hadn't liked Willa. She'd stolen Lisa Marie's fiancé and was flaunting it, rubbing her nose in it. She'd deserved a comeuppance but not to be murdered.

As we crossed the parking lot of the coffee shop, Troy was just putting his hand on Lisa Marie's head, assisting her into the backseat of a squad car. She spotted me and yelled, "Daryl Anne, I didn't do this. I swear it. You have to help me."

* * *

Hours later, my curiosity had me in a dither. I needed to know why the police had arrested Lisa Marie. Why she thought I could help her. I considered my options. Troy and the sheriff weren't going to take me into their confidences, but I had a police-connected source whom I might be able to seduce into spilling what he knew. If I played my cards right.

I arrived at Seth's house armed with the tools of a small-town seductress: a six-pack, buffalo wings, and barely there red underwear. I wasn't sure which one was happier to see me, Sonny or Seth. I suspected the buffalo wings would get the dog to hand over his secrets, but the man wouldn't be so easily duped.

Oh, I doubted I'd have little trouble getting him into bed, especially since his gaze felt spicier than the chicken I'd brought. He took in the food, the drink, and my skimpy sundress and exclaimed in a tone so sexy my lady parts tingled, "Damn, woman, did I die and go to Heaven?"

"Not yet," I said, extracting a cold beer from the carrier and twisting off the cap. "But soon…" I sidled seductively toward him, hips swaying. It was a calculated move that I'd practiced at home, learned from Hollywood temptresses I'd once known, but rehearsal hadn't included a zealous Lab darting between my legs.

I yelped and lost my balance, teetering on my too-tall high heels. I pitched forward, hand extended to stop my fall as Seth reached out to catch me. Beer spewed from the bottle like uncorked champagne, dousing him from tousled hair to bare feet. And then I slammed into him, knocking him to the floor, his strong body pillowing my impact.

I felt him quake beneath me. Oh God, had I crippled him? Broken his neck or…? Wait. Was he laughing? I pushed myself up, my gaze meeting glee-filled brown eyes. He was.

I quirked an eyebrow, grinning, my nose wrinkling. "You smell like a brewery, Quinlan."

"I thought you liked beer, Blessing."

I licked his cheek with the tip of my tongue. "I do…especially on you."

He growled and rolled me onto my back, burying his lips against mine.

Sonny barked wildly, trying to join in on the game. Seth shooed him away, but the dog wanted to wrestle with us. Giggling like children, we disentangled our limbs, sent the Lab to the backyard to chase squirrels, and headed to the bathroom. As he started the shower running, I peeled off his wet T-shirt. Seth untied the strings on my sundress, and it dropped to pool at my feet. He sucked in a sharp breath, his chocolate eyes shimmering with desire. I grazed my fingers along his flat, furred tummy and lower. The next thing I knew, my red undies landed atop his jeans, and I was in the shower, warm water streaming over me, Seth reaching for the soap.

I took the slippery bar from him and lathered my hands. I had him just where I wanted him; his secrets were no longer safe. I began spreading bubbles over his hard back, then across his delicious chest. "Did Troy tell you that he arrested Lisa Marie today?"

"Um," he said, eyes closed, head tossed back as I moved below his belt line to cup him gently.

Had he answered my question? Or was he just responding to my touches? What would Mata Hari do in this situation? Keep delving, I decided. "Did Troy tell you *why* she was arrested?"

"Umm," he said, taking the soap from me, lathering his palms, and stroking my nipples until they were so sensitive I couldn't stand it. His big hands moved to my back, to my bottom, and soon his fingers were gliding between my legs, rousing a need I'd never known I could feel.

What had I been asking him? Seth's mouth claimed mine. A moment later, he lifted my legs to wrap around his hips, and he thrust inside me, sending my thoughts away on a flood of sensation. I couldn't remember my name, let alone what I'd wanted him to tell me.

Chapter 17

As soon as the news of Lisa Marie's arrest hit the grapevine, the whole town turned into the Gossip Girls. Everyone had an opinion on the subject, facts getting skewered faster than veggies for a shish kebab. Willa Bridezilla was finally IDed as the body I'd found in the florist's cooler, the official cause of death listed as murder. The police were holding back crucial specifics, like how she'd died, which left the tongue-waggers free to come up with their own theories. I swear every possible scenario was being bandied about, from strangling to poisoning to shooting to the most bizarre—that she'd been stabbed with the cake knife from the Roosevelt wedding server set.

Was it possible to stab someone with a serrated cake knife? It seemed impossible to me, but Jenny had no trouble buying that theory.

"Apparently, the police found the matching cake slicer behind the counter at the coffee shop," she said, digging into a muffin fresh from Cold Feet Café.

"And the case," Hannah added, nodding as though she'd seen the police recover these stolen items herself.

"How do you know that?" I asked.

"Velda told me at the diner this morning when I picked up the muffins," Jenny said.

"Velda?" I choked on a laugh. That was like saying the tooth fairy told me. "You can't believe her. She makes stuff up."

But Gram seemed just as gullible as Jenny and Hannah.

"Susan," she said, "has Bernice apologized to Whitey yet, now that it's been proven he didn't steal the wedding server set?"

"What proof?" I asked, but I might as well have saved my breath. No one was listening to me.

"No," Mom said, but she didn't sound put out about it. She kept sighing and saying, "I can't stop thinking about poor Priscilla."

"I hear she's flying home today," Gram said, absently rubbing her tender wrist.

"My heart is breaking for her," Mom said. "I can't imagine that Lisa Marie could rob anything from anyone."

I was struggling with that one myself. "Did they find any wedding invitations at her home or in the coffee shop?"

Again, no one was listening to me. On the other hand, why was I asking them about the invitations? If I couldn't believe that the wedding server set was found at Pre-Wedding Jitters, how could I take their word for anything else?

Mom continued. "How could Lisa Marie do what she did to Willa?"

"She had plenty of motive," Gram said, chewing her muffin. "Oldest ones in the book. Jealousy and revenge."

"True," Mom conceded.

Okay, even I couldn't deny the motive. Willa stole her fiancé. They had that nasty fight in the coffee shop, and she did say Willa was lucky the strawberries she'd dumped on her head weren't gasoline. But I hadn't smelled gasoline in the flower shop's storeroom, nor in the cooler. No gasoline or other accelerant. Willa hadn't been killed by being burned to death. But how had she died?

I wanted to kick myself for not brushing aside those flowers like Jenny suggested and finding out for myself exactly how Willa had met her end. Even Jessica Fletcher studies the crime scene. What had I done? Barfed on it. How could I call myself a sleuth? My mind spiraled back to the moment I'd discovered the body, and the blueberry muffin I'd eaten a few minutes ago shifted uneasily in my stomach. Okay, I needed to cut myself a break. I'd reacted like almost anyone might. Hollywood just made investigating seem easy, or at least a lot easier than it was in real life.

"Is Seth here yet?" I asked, deciding I needed to discuss the Lisa Marie situation with someone who wouldn't hand me skewed facts. And without sex robbing me of my detecting senses.

"I saw him coming into the diner as I was leaving," Jenny said. "I think he was having breakfast with Officer O'Malley."

Oh yeah? A working breakfast? Could I risk intruding? Is Meg's hair red?

I was tired of crazy speculation and unfounded gossip. I wanted actual facts, *straight from the horse's mouth*, as Gram was fond of saying. I already tried seducing the truth out of Seth, but I'd only managed to realize that I'd never make it as a temptress spy. The outcome of my stab at being Mata Hari, however, made me eager to see him. I sighed, remembering. Note to self: *Keep your mind on the mission. 'Cause that had worked so well last night.*

"I'll be back before we open," I told Mom, and then took off for Cold Feet Café. The day promised to be another scorcher, the temperature already in the seventies at eight a.m. I hurried along, keeping my eyes toward the ground, not wanting to get stopped or to engage in more speculative notions about Lisa Marie and Willa Bridezilla. I'd been avoiding random encounters with townsfolk since finding the body, and I knew there were at least three Curious Cathys who'd love to catch me alone and pump me for "the scoop."

I arrived at the café without encountering them, breathing a sigh of relief, and was drawn inside by the tantalizing aroma of frying food. I hadn't realized until my stomach reacted to the delicious odors that half of a sugar-free muffin wasn't enough fuel to get me through until lunch.

I hadn't considered, however, how packed the café would be. There wasn't even an empty stool at the counter. I should've known, given it was gossip central and the only place to get a decent cup of coffee, now that Pre-Wedding Jitters was temporarily closed.

I spied Meg's fiery hair way in the back and hoped she was seated with Troy and Seth. I purposefully didn't meet anyone's gaze or acknowledge a single "good morning, Daryl Anne" with more than a nod of my head. Two booths from Meg, I heard Velda cry out, "Daryl Anne, we need to talk."

I felt as though she'd poked a knife in my back. I kept walking, didn't turn around. I pretended I hadn't heard her, although I was certain everyone in the café had. I quickly slipped into the booth across from Meg, realizing only as my fanny hit the cushion that she was not sitting and chatting with her fiancé or my boyfriend but a different man altogether. He was shorter than Troy and Seth by a few inches, fairly good-looking in a leading man's best friend kind of way.

I blurted out, "Dillon, what are you doing here?"

"Good morning to you, too, Daryl Anne." Dillon Farwell had the weary blue eyes and weak smile of a man who'd had little sleep and was overly stressed about something. Like the murder of his beloved fiancée. His black dyed hair gave his pale face a sickly hue. I reminded myself to be kinder. After all, he was grieving.

"I'm sorry for your loss," I said, my voice gentle and calm, while inside I was dealing with a myriad mixed emotions. After all, I'd found the body, and he might want details. I hadn't come here to relive the worst moment of my life but to get some facts. Hard, cold facts. *Cold. Cold, cold flesh. Damn.* Would that memory continue to randomly pop to mind forever?

Dillon stared at his coffee as though some dark wisdom were written there. "It's definitely a tough time for Willa's family and friends and…everyone."

No matter my dislike of the tiny brunette, I had to remember that Dillon had loved her. "And you."

He cringed as if I'd suggested he eat worms, and then another strange emotion passed through his eyes, as if he had a guilty secret that he ached to confess but couldn't quite find the words.

I glanced questioningly at Meg. Had he shared with her what was bothering him? "So, what's going on, you two?"

She ordered me a cup of coffee, and after it arrived and I'd taken possession of it, she said, "Dillon has been telling me something rather interesting."

"Oh, yeah?" I looked from one to the other.

"I think you should tell her, Dillon," Meg urged.

He pushed against the back of the cushion and made a face that said he didn't like repeating himself. Or maybe it meant he regretted having told Meg. I said, "She'll just tell me later if you don't tell me now, Dillon."

I could see he knew it was true. He took a quick gulp of coffee, then blurted out, "Lisa Marie didn't steal our wedding invitations from Zelda's. I did."

I almost spit coffee at him. "What? Why?"

His sigh could've been heard to the front door, but then he leaned closer to me, lowering his voice. "I didn't want Willa and her mother to send them."

I said, "I don't understand."

"It was a mistake. The whole thing. Sure I was flattered by the attention she paid me when we met at my casino concert." *Did I forget to mention that Dillon is an Elvis impersonator? A pretty good one by all accounts, when he isn't working in his father's grocery store.* He scratched his forehead. "The one-night stand led to another and another. I'm not proud of myself, but she's, er, she was persuasive, you know?"

I could imagine.

He went on. "Before I knew it, Willa was demanding I break it off with Lisa Marie and marry her."

"It didn't hurt that she was a trust-fund baby," Meg said, the comment cutting.

If he was after sympathy, he wasn't getting it from me either. Cheaters suck. *If you're in a relationship with one person but find yourself more attracted to another, then do the honorable thing and extricate yourself from the first relationship before diving into the next.* "Go on."

His ears were a little red. "Hey, I admit that her being rich played into my decision-making. But who could blame me? I figured I could quit the grocery store and devote myself full-time to my music career."

I understood ambition, but what kind of longevity did an Elvis impersonator realistically have? The waitress showed up to refill our coffee, and I ordered a Big Finn special, eggs over easy, crisp bacon, crunchy hash browns, and wheat toast.

"Tell her the rest, Dillon," Meg said.

"Willa's father had other ideas. He wanted me to learn his business, starting in the mail room."

A fit punishment for dumping Lisa Marie.

"Like I hadn't put up with enough of that old-man shit from my own old man," Dillon grumbled, and fell into a brooding mood, glaring out the window at a seagull perched on a nearby piling.

My food arrived, and I dug in, mixing the eggs and hash browns with a dollop of ketchup. As I munched a piece of bacon, I mulled over what Dillon had said and realized he hadn't once mentioned the L-word while speaking about Willa. Why? I eyed him curiously, wondering if his distress was about his fiancée's demise, as I'd assumed when I sat down, or about something else altogether. "So what are you saying?"

"I told Willa I wasn't going to marry her."

Definitely about something else. "When did you break up with her?"

"Weeks ago."

I frowned, chewing my eggs and potatoes as well as what this meant. "Then why was Willa still planning the wedding?"

Dillon narrowed his eyes. "She said I was not going to humiliate her or her family."

Meg rolled her eyes. "Did you tell her to get over it?"

"No. I didn't dare."

"What does that mean?" I asked, slathering jam on my toast.

"Her father said I'd made a commitment to his daughter, and by God, I would live up to it or live to regret it."

"He threatened you?" Meg's eyes rounded.

Dillon nodded. "To sue me for breach of promise and include my whole family, who were not fond of Willa, in the lawsuit."

I gulped. Willa's dad had lawyers at his beck and call. Dillon's family could lose everything.

"Wow, she was worse than I thought, and I thought she was pretty bad," Meg muttered.

Dillon smirked. "I told her dad to go to hell."

"Pretty brave of you," I said, wondering if he'd thought that decision through.

"Didn't do any good," he said, his tone suggesting Willa was one crazy bitch. "She kept planning and ordering stuff for the wedding. As though it were still on. She meant to send those invitations."

"Why?" Meg shrugged. "It's not like you were going to show up at the church."

"She and her old man actually figured I would and that I'd marry her as planned."

"Wow," Meg said.

Dillon shook his head, that weary expression taking hold of him again. "I couldn't get rid of her."

I was thinking someone had done Dillon a favor by offing Willa. Like maybe Dillon. My food turned to pebbles in my stomach. Lisa Marie's motive for killing Willa was powerful, but not nearly as powerful as his. Were Meg and I sitting with the real bridezilla killer? I shoved my plate away from me.

"Meg and Daryl Anne," Dillon said, "I have a huge favor to ask you."

I didn't like the sound of this. Was he intending to pick my brain for details of the crime scene to ensure he hadn't left any clues that would point to him, instead of Lisa Marie, as the killer? I said a leery, "Okay?"

"The sheriff is wrong about Lisa Marie," he said. "She didn't kill Willa."

Oh God, maybe he was going to confess. Maybe he wanted us to go with him to the police station as he turned himself in.

Wait. Why would he want that? My nerves were scrambling my common sense.

Dillon was looking at me strangely, as if trying to read my expression. He said, "She wants you to visit her in jail."

My last image of Lisa Marie flashed into my mind, her words as fresh as if she were yelling at me now: *"Daryl Anne, I didn't do this. I swear it. You have to help me."* Why had she said that? What help did she think I had to give her? Did she imagine I could actually solve a crime like Rick Castle? Because she was wrong. I'd never once had Lisa Marie on my suspect list. I sure hadn't thought of her as a killer either. Even if the victim was the bitch who stole Dillon. Wait. Maybe the fact that I'd never suspected her was exactly why she thought I could help. I really did believe she was innocent. Why? For one thing, she'd seemed to be coming around to the idea that if Willa hadn't stolen Dillon, someone else would've. And that wiped out any jealousy/revenge motive.

"Why does she want to see us?" Meg asked.

He rubbed his jaw. "She says, you know, when your mom was killed, well, you and Daryl Anne solved the murder."

"That's not technically true," Meg said.

Although we had *tried* to solve it.

Dillon wasn't giving up. "She said Daryl Anne is good at unraveling things to get to the truth."

I am? If that's true, and I'm not saying it is, then maybe he should worry I'll come up with proof that he killed Willa.

"Come on, Daryl Anne," Meg said. "What harm will it do to hear what Lisa Marie wants to tell us?"

Famous last words.

Chapter 18

There's something so satisfying about helping a woman find a dress that suits her body type, enhances her curves, and makes her feel as beautiful as every bride should at her wedding. Getting to that point isn't always easy, however. Too often the bride can't set aside long-held body issues and see what is reflected in the mirror, no matter how many supporters ooh and aah or even shed happy tears. And too often, not everyone in a bride's shopping entourage has her best interests at heart and criticizes every choice until the bride is confused and disheartened, no longer trusting her own instincts or dreams.

Turns out my day job isn't much different than that of being maid of honor. Keep the bride calm. And smiling.

For the most part, I'd managed that today. But now the shop was closed, the customers gone, and my feet hurt. On the downside, I'd wrestled jealous best friends, skinflint fathers, spoiled mama's girls, and one ornery grandmother. The latter was my own. Billie could slice a tiara in half with the glare she was giving me. I'd caught her hand stitching seed pearls onto a special order gown. A definite no-no. The doctor had forbidden any handwork, as it would hamper the healing process of her wrist.

She lifted her chin, defiance in the set of her shoulders. "If I can't do this, Daryl Anne, you might as well put me out to pasture. I can't sit around this shop twiddling my thumbs." She shook her head. "Nope. I'm not allowed to do that either. I'm not allowed to do anything. I can't use the computer, so I can't do the bookwork. I can't lift the gowns from the racks. I can't log in the gowns in the storeroom, freeing up Hannah to work with shoppers. I'm just a worthless old woman without any purpose."

Now my heart hurt as well as my feet. My earliest memories were of Billie buried in a pile of snowy lace, stitching sequins onto a princess ball gown that seemed to have stepped from the pages of my bedtime storybook. That day I'd imagined my grammy was a fairy godmother with magic wand fingers. She could transform a plain dress into one fit for a queen. I knew then that I wanted to do the same. And so she taught me.

I pulled her into a bear hug. "Oh, Gram, I'm sorry, darling. I know this is frustrating, but you're the strongest woman I know. My all-time hero. The wrist needs a vacation, and you could use one, too. The expo will be over in a couple more days and—"

"I can't take a vacation." She stepped back, eyeing me as if I'd lost my mind.

"Then a night out with some of your gal pals. Isn't it bingo night at the casino?"

"Yes," she conceded, the sadness filling her eyes again. "But they've left by now."

"I'll drop you off, Billie," Seth said, coming into alterations, no doubt drawn there by the sound of our voices. "I'm doing a wedding tonight in Tacoma. I'll be passing right by the casino."

She brightened at that. "If you're sure it's no trouble?"

"No trouble at all," he assured her.

"I need time to change my top and freshen my hair and makeup. Ten minutes tops."

"Perfect," Seth grinned as she hustled off to the elevator with a new lightness in her step.

I moved toward him, smiling, wondering what I'd done to deserve such a great, caring guy. "Thank you for that. She's really struggling with the thought of another surgery and more time off to heal again."

"Yeah, I could tell. And I am going that way. In fact, Blessing"—he touched my cheek—"the offer still stands for you, if you want to tag along."

"I'm sorry." As much as I wanted to accept, I couldn't. Meg had wrangled us a visitation with Lisa Marie at the jail. "I have a meet-up with my own gal pal that can't be canceled."

"Next time, then." He pulled me into his arms and kissed me, and I admit to seriously considering canceling on Meg. Seth eased back, peering at me. "But I'll be thinking about you all evening."

"I won't be with Meg all night, you know."

His laugh was throaty and sexy and sent shivers of want through me. He said, "I was hoping you'd say that."

* * *

Last time I'd been to the jail, I was almost tossed into a cell for screaming at Sheriff Gooden. Okay, maybe it was *almost* an assault on a police officer. Meg saved me from incarceration, so it was probably good that she was with me now. Just in case.

"Are you sure we have to go to the police station to see Lisa Marie? Maybe we could wait until she makes bail?" I asked.

"Apparently she's waiting for her mother to get home and handle that. Priscilla is bringing some big-deal legal eagle to take over the case from the court-appointed guy."

"What's our hurry, then?"

She arched a pointed brow that spoke volumes of silent reprimand. "Daryl Anne Blessing, she wants to tell us something ASAP."

I still didn't want to go into the jail, but curiosity overcame my reluctance. "Okay."

"We won't have much time with her," she warned.

"We should figure out what to ask her now, then," I said.

"I want to know why she took my ring." Meg's lips were a flat line of disapproval. "If she hadn't, it wouldn't be sitting in the evidence room but on my finger where it belongs. I mean, just because her engagement didn't work out doesn't mean she has a right to ruin others' weddings."

I think my eyebrows might have disappeared into the stratosphere. "I didn't know she'd been identified as the Weddingville thief. Were the stolen items found at her place? Did Troy tell you that?"

Meg blinked. "Well, no, but it's what everyone is saying."

"Everyone?" Exasperation spiked through me. "Gossips, you mean?"

"I guess." She had the decency to look ashamed of herself. Meg bit her bottom lip and blinked again. "I just assumed..."

"I think half the town is assuming, but remember what happened when Mom was arrested. Everyone jumped to conclusions, believing that an arrest is all the proof needed to convict. Condemning her without all the facts. I'm not sure we have all the facts now either."

"Okay, then we'll only ask Lisa Marie about the murder."

"Agreed." I reached for the door and minutes later, we were seated in a tiny visitor room about the size of a walk-in closet, a guard standing rigid at the door.

Truth be told, I'd rather be anywhere but here. One look at Lisa Marie convinced me that she felt the same. The bubbly, smart-mouthed young woman we knew resembled a bedraggled street person, her hair flat and matted, wearing a shapeless jumpsuit, no makeup or jewelry, and desperation her new perfume. My heart went out to her. Although I still wasn't sure why she wanted to see us. Or me.

"Thank you for coming." Her voice was scratchy, her eyes puffy, as if she'd been nonstop crying.

Keeping in mind the time limit, Meg charged ahead. "We talked to Dillon."

"Then you know." Lisa Marie's shoulders slumped as if in relief.

I wasn't sure how Lisa Marie had leaped to that conclusion, but Meg and I exchanged a confused glance. I shook my head. "No, we don't."

"I didn't kill that woman. Didn't he tell you that? I had no reason."

"Was, ah, is Dillon trying to get back together with you?" Meg asked, leading me to wonder what this had to do with the murder.

"God, is that what he told you?" Lisa Marie twisted her hands, emitting a sound like a small animal growl. "Yes, yes, he is. But I'm not interested. Willa did me a favor."

"Favor?" I asked before Meg cut off the opportunity. "I thought you and Dillon were in love."

She shook her head. "The only reason we started dating was because our moms are friends. They both belong to the King

Sisters, you know? They've told us since we were kids how cool it would be if Dillon and I ended up married. I like Dillon. He's a fun guy. And we were young, so we drank our Mom's Kool-Aid. When he decided to become an Elvis impersonator and started playing gigs, it was exciting. It was also like an extension of my mom's obsession. The relationship became reliable."

Familiar, I thought.

"Safe," Meg said.

"Exactly." Lisa Marie nodded. "After he dumped me for Willa, though, I realized I didn't miss him all that much. Or at all, really. In fact, while Mom's been away, I started dating this other guy, who doesn't even like Elvis, and he's pretty wonderful."

Meg pursed her lips. "Why didn't you tell Willa that before tossing strawberries at her?"

"Would you have told her anything if she came at you like that? She threw coffee in my face. And she wouldn't stop shrieking."

I had to admit the coffee in the face was over the top and uncalled for. There was no denying Willa's inflated sense of entitlement. The question was, had it gotten her killed?

Lisa Marie twisted her hands tighter. "After I cooled down, I decided it would be safest for the coffee shop and my well-being if I just told her that I wasn't out to destroy her wedding. Or break up her engagement. I wish now that I'd decided not to tell her in person."

"Why?" I asked.

"I, er, I saw her go into the Flower Girl that morning. I caught up with her inside and told her that she could have Dillon. I was glad he was marrying her. I didn't want him. Instead of making her happy, this seemed to upset her. She turned red in the face, called me a couple of names, and waved her hands. I left before she started throwing plants at me. I swear, the last I saw of her, she was still alive and standing. I didn't have any reason to kill her."

My stomach sank. We only had Lisa Marie's word that she had no motive for murder, and she could be lying. She'd just given us means and opportunity and supplied the reason for her arrest.

Meg asked, "Did anyone see you with Willa at the flower shop?"

"A witness, you mean?" Lisa Marie shrugged. "I didn't notice anybody watching us. But there were a lot of shoppers in the store. If there was a witness, surely they'd have seen that I didn't touch Willa."

"But if there were no witnesses, how did the police jump to you as the prime suspect?" Someone must have seen them together; otherwise the cops wouldn't have arrested her on supposition.

"I don't know," Lisa Marie said. "Maybe Velda or Jeanette told them about what happened at the coffee shop."

"If that was the reason you were arrested, Troy would've questioned Daryl Anne and me," Meg said. "But he didn't."

Lisa Marie sighed. "But if someone witnessed me and Willa arguing in the floral shop, wouldn't the police need to tell my lawyer that?"

I nodded. *Full disclosure is a thing, right?* "I think it's a law."

"Well, they didn't."

"They must have something connecting you to the murder, Lisa Marie, or you wouldn't be in a cell. The DA needs actual evidence to go to trial. A witness or DNA or something else tangible." *You only need to watch an episode of* Law & Order *to know that.* "My attorney said they found part of my name tag on the body."

I blanched, recalling the fisted hand rising from the flowers. So that's what she'd been clutching.

Meg's eyes were as huge as saucers. "Did she rip it off you during the struggle?"

"What struggle?" Lisa Marie frowned, her voice rising. "I told you we didn't fight. She just started making threats about alienation of affection, and I got the hell away from her."

"She was hardly in a position to sue you for alienation of affection." Meg looked indignant. "She stole Dillon from you first."

"I didn't steal him back. I don't want him back."

"If Willa didn't rip the name tag from you, how did it end up with her body?" Meg said.

"The name tag the police have is one I tossed out last week. The clasp broke. I didn't notice that it had dropped to the floor, and I stepped on it, snapping it in two. I tossed it in the garbage at the coffee shop."

"Then how did it end up with Willa?" *Clutched in her tiny fist?*

Lisa Marie flopped back against the chair, her head moving slightly from side to side, a lost, helpless expression on her face. "I don't know."

"How would anyone even know you'd tossed it out?" Meg scrunched her face and lifted her hands toward the ceiling, as if seeking an answer from the divine. And apparently coming up with an idea. "Did you mention it to a customer at the time, or did a customer see it happen?"

Lisa Marie sat a little straighter, grasping at this lifeline, thin as it might be. Chances were good someone had been in the shop at the time. Her business had a pretty steady stream of coffee drinkers. She said, "You think the killer took the name tag from the garbage when I wasn't paying attention?"

"Isn't that possible?" I asked, knowing she didn't stay behind the counter all the time but often visited with her customers at their tables.

She tilted her head, considering it. "I suppose."

Meg said, "Who was there that day?"

Lisa Marie groaned. "Who's there every day? Regulars. One day runs into another. You know how that goes."

Meg might be able to relate to that. She practically grew up in her dad's café with regular customers day in and day out. But I couldn't. The bridal shop didn't have daily repeat clientele. It was pretty easy for me to recall which customer had come in on which day.

"Think," I said, recalling something I'd seen on one of my favorite crime shows. "Let your mind clear and picture yourself in the coffee shop, walk yourself through your routine, then stop at the point when you step on the name tag. You feel that plastic snap beneath your shoe. Now look around the coffee shop. Who's there?"

Lisa Marie closed her eyes, silently following my instructions, but the door to the visitor room bumped open, startling us all, stealing the moment.

Sheriff Gooden stood there, his scowl as dark as midnight. "Who authorized this visit?"

Once again, Meg had to drag me out of the police station before I shamed the name of Blessing.

Chapter 19

The Last Fling was packed; the only seating left was two stools at the bar. Meg and I grabbed them. Her phone went off as we sat down. I eyed her with surprise and then realized this was another sign that she was regaining control of her life. She pulled the phone from her purse and read the screen. "It's a text from Troy."

I settled on the bar stool and ordered our drinks, thinking to give her some privacy, but she said, "I texted him about Lisa Marie."

"Did you tell him what she told us?" We weren't attorneys sworn to confidentiality by law, but still it felt disloyal to disclose the conversation to the people trying to pin a murder charge on her.

"No. Although, what harm could it do? All she told us was that she's innocent."

"True."

"I asked Troy if he, the sheriff, or the DA thought Lisa Marie was the Weddingville thief."

I paid for our drinks and slid hers toward her. "And you actually think he'll tell you that?"

"Why not, if they don't?"

Why not? Because it was an official police investigation. "I bet I know exactly how he responded to that. 'Keep your nosy little nose out of my case,' right?"

"Actually, it was 'pretty little nose.'" She laughed. "But I texted back that I had a victim's right to know and that I wouldn't tell anyone else. Not even you. So you didn't hear this from me, okay? Promise."

"I swear on my daddy's grave."

She leaned closer, glancing right and left, and held her phone for me to read Troy's response: *None of the still missing, stolen items were found at the coffee shop or at her apartment or her mom's house.*

I met Meg's gaze. She said, "You were right."

She deleted the message from her phone.

"I just never pegged Lisa Marie as a thief. Burglar. Robber. Whichever it is."

"None of the above." Meg chuckled.

A tiny stone of concern seemed to lift from my heart, and I realized I believed Lisa Marie was innocent of murder, too. Otherwise, I wouldn't be worrying about her. Or thinking that there had to be something I could do to help her. But what? And then I had an idea.

"If I'm brave enough to dish out advice, I should be strong enough to take it, right?" I asked.

"Sure," Meg said, scooting her stool closer to the bar and sipping her drink, a Honeymoon Sweet Irish Coffee, light on the Irish and heavy on the whipped cream. "What advice is that?"

I'd needed something stronger than what she was having. It was the first time I'd tried a Blue Diamond, some concoction with gin, champagne, and Curaçao, a liqueur that tasted a bit like oranges and gave the cocktail its royal hue. It was refreshing with a kick and was probably turning my tongue and gums blue. "Remember I asked Lisa Marie to close her eyes and walk through the moment when she'd stepped on the name tag, to stop and look, to see what she hadn't noticed or noted at the time?"

"I thought that was really clever. It might've worked, too, if Sheriff Gooden hadn't butted in."

Just his name raised my hackles. I tamped down the irritation, concentrating on what I was saying. "I should do the same thing with the crime scene. You know, walk myself through without any emotion. Maybe I'll recall something important. Something that might point to another suspect."

"You think she's innocent?"

"Don't you?"

"I no longer trust my bullshit meter." Meg lifted her thick hair off her neck. "But I still trust yours. She seemed believable. But I got the impression that Dillon thought she was going to take him back. So that bit about some new guy she's dating kind of threw me."

"That's something that can be checked out," I said. Once Lisa Marie was bailed out of jail and we could get the man's name. I wasn't risking another visit to the police station. "It seems to me, at the moment, that Dillon had more reason than anyone to kill Willa."

Meg shook her head. "I've known him forever. He's not hotheaded or violent."

"Anyone pushed hard enough will push back at some point. And Willa and her father were human bulldozers backing him to the edge of a cliff." Could Dillon have snapped under the pressure and killed Willa? I kept coming back to the same stumbling block. "It would really help if we knew how she'd been murdered."

"I've tried finagling it out of Troy, but he's staying as mum as a mummy."

I closed my eyes, tuning out the music and voices in the bar, and tried the exercise I'd recommended to Lisa Marie.

I see the storeroom as it was when I entered. I glance around. The only sign of disturbance is the steamed glass in the largest cooler. I approach. My gaze goes to the smaller cooler. Flowers and plants. Nothing of note. I gaze toward the large cooler and feel uneasiness begin to stir inside me. I swallow hard, restraining the panic that wants me to open my eyes and end this walk down memory lane. I force myself onward. I'm struck by something odd. There is no sign of the devastation inside the cooler from this side. Not so much as a shard of glass on the floor by the door. A rose petal. A twig. All the destruction and chaos are contained within, hidden by the fogged glass.

I opened my eyes. Meg was staring at me like she used to when I played guinea pig to her cooking skills. A little eager, a little fretful. "Did it work?"

I nodded, kind of amazed that it had. I filled Meg in on what I'd recalled, then said with conviction, "She wasn't shot."

"How can you be sure?"

"Several reasons. With all of the theories flying around, no one has said anything about hearing a gunshot. Not even Flora. She brought up my screams but not a word about a loud bang."

"You're right. I haven't heard anyone at the diner mention hearing a gunshot either." Meg licked whipped cream from her upper lip.

"Next, the lack of gore. We know from forensic shows that when someone is shot there's always blowback or blood splatter. But there was none of that."

"What about a bullet hole in the cooler?"

I shook my head. "Nope. No telltale odor either."

"What odor?"

"You know, the smell that firing a gun causes."

"Can't say I've ever smelled that."

Neither had I, but all I recalled was the scent of roses and greens and a slightly funky odor that I assumed was dead body. "We need a copy of the autopsy report."

"Fat chance." Meg's brow creased. "How will knowing the cause of death help us figure out who killed her?"

The crowd noise was increasing, I realized, as I had to lean in to hear this last question. I was suddenly aware that we could be overheard, and I squirmed, glancing around to see if anyone was listening to our conversation. "Maybe we should take this somewhere more private."

Meg ignored that. "I've been thinking that Willa was put in the cooler to conceal the time of death." She watched TV mysteries, too, and she'd even done the makeup on one of the *CSI* franchise shows. She knew things even I didn't.

"If I hadn't arrived when I did to pick up the roses for the bridal shop, and if Flora hadn't been too busy to have them at the counter, the body might not have been discovered until late in the day."

Meg nodded. "Which would've given the killer time to come up with a solid alibi."

I thought about this as I sipped my drink. "Whoever killed her planned it."

"I agree. Why else would someone take that name tag if not to frame Lisa Marie?"

"That means when Lisa Marie followed Willa into the flower shop, the killer followed after her, later taking advantage of the second argument and somehow luring Willa into the storeroom."

"Yep." Meg slurped the last of her drink.

I gulped down the rest of my own. "We should question Flora and Violet."

"The Flower Girl will be closed for the night by now."

"Tomorrow, then." We abandoned our drinks and started walking back toward Front Street. Dusk cast shadows along the route. Streetlights didn't exist this far away from the main area of town, and a soft wind rustled through the leaves of trees, giving me shivers. It wasn't cold. It was the talk of murder that had me a bit edgy. But do you think I could get my mind on something else? *Hell no.* "Who do you think might've wanted Willa dead?"

"Gee, she was such a sweetheart, I can't imagine," Meg said. "Unless you mean everyone unfortunate enough to come in contact with her."

"That's not helping."

"Sorry, I calls 'em like I sees 'em."

"I was hoping to narrow the suspect pool, not make it as large as Puget Sound." I rubbed the back of my neck as a creepy uneasiness swept over me again. It wasn't a feeling like we were in imminent danger, but more like a foreboding. As if something bad was going to happen. Soon. Maybe I should leave the detecting to the detectives and stop scaring myself.

I decided to switch to another topic that was bugging me. "So, have you made any decisions regarding your wedding?"

Like are you going through with it?

"Wow, talk about shifting gears."

"Well…"

She gave a soft laugh. "I have. And I hope it will make you as happy as it's making me."

Anticipation swept through me, shoving the uneasiness aside. "What's going on?"

Meg said, "This past week showed me that putting something off for a better time or the right time or until all the stars are aligned in the heavens is just plain risky. Life is fragile and susceptible to crazy influences. I need to grab what's strong in my life and go for it. With or without Granny O's ring."

"Oh my God, that's wonderful!" I grabbed her and hugged her. "What time frame are we looking at? Do you have a date?"

"As soon as we can manage. Troy and I have an appointment with Reverend Bell tomorrow morning to arrange the date and hour."

"Why didn't you tell me sooner?"

"I wasn't going to tell you until the expo ends. You've got enough stress, worrying about Billie, trying to help Lisa Marie. The whole upset of finding Willa."

"Nothing is as important as your wedding. In fact, what are you doing out with me tonight when you should be with your fiancé, confirming plans?"

"He's looking into a lead on the robberies tonight."

"A lead? A serious lead? That's great." A surge of anticipation swelled in me. I wanted every detail but had to bank the excitement since I knew I wouldn't get anything. "I know, I know, you can't tell me anything about it. Darn it."

She hesitated.

"What?" Why did I feel like I wasn't going to like her answer?

"He's...ah...Look, don't be mad at me, okay? I told him what Hannah had said about it seeming like the thief was stealing a wedding. He called her, and she asked him to meet her at the bridal shop tonight to discuss it. She wanted to show him something she thought seemed odd."

My uneasy feeling crept from the shadows and raised goose bumps on my limbs. *My strange cousin and her stranger ways.*

"What could something at the bridal shop have to do with the robberies?"

"I have no idea." We'd reached Front Street and turned toward Blessing's. "He didn't give me any details other than that."

"I suppose I'll have to ask Hannah." My curiosity meter was pinging like a smoke alarm. If I went straight to the shop right now—

"Meg!" a male voice called.

We turned to find Dillon jogging up the sidewalk toward us with the gait of a couch potato. He caught up, bent over, and gasped for breath. "I've been trying to find you. I just came from the jail."

"Did you get in to see Lisa Marie?" Meg asked.

"Nah. The sheriff was being a prick. But her attorney was just coming out. He wouldn't help me get in to see her either, but he gave me this note to give to you, Daryl Anne."

Dillon handed me a sealed, plain white envelope. I wasn't sure that I should open it with him there. Waiting, however, was not an option. I moved to stand under a streetlamp and slid my finger through the upper flap. It contained a single sheet of paper with printed lettering in pencil.

I remembered. Some of the temps, who are working the shops during the expo, were at a couple of the tables. Hannah was also there. Lurking. Watching me.

"Hannah was there," I said to Meg.

"Your cousin?" Dillon said. "Where is 'there'? What does that mean?"

"Nothing." I didn't want him to say anything against Hannah that might be repeated and thrashed through the town gossip machine.

Meg seemed pale, as if her creatively applied makeup had washed away with the tide. Maybe it was the lighting. Maybe I was misreading her alarm. But then she grasped my arm so hard, I knew I wasn't mistaken.

"We have to go, Dillon," she said, tugging me up the street. "See you later."

We hurried away from him, moving at a quick clip toward the bridal shop. "Troy's alone with her."

I wanted to deny that Troy was in danger. Hannah wasn't a killer, was she? What would she have had against Willa Bridezilla? "Let's not jump to conclusions, Meg. Lisa Marie said there were other temps there that day, not just Hannah. And even if she is the killer, she has nothing to fear from Troy. She thinks Lisa Marie's arrest will keep her safe. Why would she harm Troy?"

"She's always been a few pencil strokes shy of a full eyebrow."

I couldn't argue with that, or quell the urgency that was eating at me.

"I'll feel better when I see Troy," Meg said.

His police sedan was parked at the back of the shop.

I unlocked the door, and we stepped inside. The lights in the office area were turned off, including the night-lights. My pulse wobbled.

"Where is everyone?" Meg whispered.

"Mom's out with Whitey, and Gram's at the casino playing bingo."

"I mean, Troy and Hannah."

Of course she did. I spotted a light beyond alterations in the warehouse where the shipments arrived. "This way," I whispered.

We stepped as silently as possible. My heart seemed to want to crack my ribs and escape. I was sure Meg could hear it, unless her own pulse was roaring in her ears. We emerged into a ten-by-twenty area with brick walls, a bay for deliveries. Metal dress racks and cardboard boxes dominated the space. This was Hannah's domain. She logged in the shipments when they arrived, accounting for each dress on the invoices and ordering new gowns as needed. A secondhand desk stood against the wall, a service lamp the only light source.

"Where are they?" Meg whispered, fear cracking her voice.

"I don't know." I strained to hear a sound, not sure which direction to head next. And then I spotted one of the racks. It had been overturned as though something hard was knocked into it.

"What the hell went on in here?" Panic had joined the fear in Meg's voice.

I didn't want her to know I was just as scared. Plastic-wrapped gowns were scattered across the concrete floor. I thanked God for the protective coverings, but a large spray of blood on one of the zippered bags nearly stopped my heartbeat.

"Listen," Meg said, grabbing my hand.

I heard it then. Muted sounds coming from the main salon. Chanting or singing. I couldn't make out which. I only knew something was wrong. Very, very wrong. I pointed toward the landline on the desk. "Call 9-1-1, Meg."

"Wait." Meg caught my arm, digging into her purse. "You need a weapon."

She slapped something into my palm that looked a little like brass knuckles, only it was plastic. "What is this?"

"It's a Zap Blast Knuckles stun gun. Nine hundred fifty thousand volts. Daddy had Troy take me to buy this after we were attacked by my mother's killer. It's great for jogging and fits in my purse." She gave me rapid-fire, how-to instructions and turned toward the phone.

I shoved my fingers through the slots, the device weighty on my knuckles. Feeling armed and dangerous, I gathered my courage and hastened to the salon. Memories of facing down Meg's mother's killer swamped me. My feet felt like sandbags. My brain screamed for me to wait for the police. To let them handle it. But then I pictured the blood on the plastic bag and a worse fear gripped me. What if Hannah had hurt Troy? I was praying Meg hadn't leaped to that same conclusion, deciding to follow me, because there was no predicting what she'd do.

I wasn't sure what I thought I could do. But I had to do something.

I stole to the edge of the salon and froze at the sound of someone humming the wedding march. I peered into the room. My eyes widened. It had been transformed into a makeshift chapel. Folding chairs, usually stored in the warehouse, faced a podium. The window mannequins were seated on either side of a red carpet runner. Every drop of liquid left my mouth. A lone mannequin remained in the display window. Seth's photo posters were aligned to block the glass from the view of outside passersby.

Candles were everywhere. Rose petals strewn here and there. Troy was slumped in a folding chair in the groom's spot. Hannah wore a puffy Cinderella wedding dress, a glittery tiara securing a heavy veil that hid her face. She was softly humming "Here Comes the Bride."

A low moan touched my ear. I guessed it was coming from Troy. *Please don't let his injury be serious. Or life-threatening. Meg can't lose him, too.*

"Do you have any idea how long I've waited for this moment, my love?" Hannah said, her voice different. Deranged.

She grasped Troy by the hair, moving his head as if he were nodding. He groaned. Still alive. But I winced and glanced away, my gaze landing on the desk that Seth was using during the expo. His brochures had been removed. A wedding cake stood in the center with an antique wedding server set beside it. The missing Roosevelt set? My hands grew slick. I nearly dropped the stun gun.

"Something old, something new, something borrowed, something blue." She held her hand up to the light. "This beautiful diamond ring covers it all. It's new to me, it's old, it's borrowed, and it's blue. Perfect. Like us. Like our wedding. Like our love."

I had to get closer, close enough to press the stun-knuckle-thingy against her skin. I fisted my hand, trying to keep it on my sweaty fingers. As I crouched and crept toward the makeshift altar, I heard a whimper from the display window. A chill shot through me. I jerked sideways. Horror slammed into me as I realized what I hadn't noticed previously. It wasn't a mannequin in a wedding gown in the display window but a woman in a long light-colored summer dress. A dark liquid stain was spreading across her bodice. Blood. I began to shake. I lifted my gaze higher and saw the ashen face of my cousin.

"Hannah," I gasped. The bride at the altar heard me.

She spun around. She grabbed the knife from the server set. The blade dripped blood. I yelped as she tore toward me with the speed of a bat, the blade extended. I dropped the stun knuckles. They landed with a thump on the carpet. I dove to retrieve my weapon. Next thing I knew I was on the floor, fighting for my life. Screaming. The tip of the knife touched my throat. I struggled harder. She was stronger than me. *Searing pain. Hot liquid trickling down my neck. Blood.* I was going to die.

Meg charged in, scooped up the stun knuckles, and jammed the weapon against my assailant's wrist. Insane Bride shrieked and collapsed on me like a dead bear.

I gasped, and the world went black.

Chapter 20

There are times when withholding information in order to catch a murderer is the wrong tactic. If someone would've told me that Willa's closed fist had held a button and not Lisa Marie's name tag, I could've supplied a prime suspect. But no one told me. No one asked me. And I am still a little sore. No, I'm not angry. I'm hurting from the cut to my neck and the bruises from the fight with Insane Bride.

It turned out that Willa had been stabbed, the same as Hannah, with the knife from the wedding server set. The killer had ground down the serrated edges, honing the blade to a deadly sharpness. Although I still reeled from almost being killed, I hadn't ended up in the hospital or the morgue. Others were not as lucky.

Mom, Billie, and I clustered together in the ICU waiting room the next morning. Okay, so I had ended up in the hospital. Just not as a patient. Hannah, however, was in dire trouble. She'd had to be stabilized before they could operate on the life-threatening puncture to her abdomen. She'd lost a lot of blood. They'd finally wheeled her into surgery an hour ago.

We'd been up most of the night and were all pretty frazzled. Mom couldn't stop blaming herself. "I checked Jenny's references personally," she kept saying, as if she'd set a mad dog loose in Weddingville.

I tried to reason with her. "The references were real. She stole Jenny Carson's identity."

"I should've asked the Veiled Bride for a photo ID." She stared at her untouched coffee cup, the liquid cold for more than an hour now. "I should've asked..."

"Mom, this isn't your fault."

"But Hannah and Troy..." She burst into tears.

"Troy's okay." Seth came through the door at that moment, catching the last of Mom's self-recrimination.

I'd never been more glad to see anyone. I rushed into his arms, and he held me close, absorbing my lingering fear and silently letting me know he was my safe haven. He studied me a long moment, checking out the bandage on my neck. "Are you all right, Blessing?"

"A little scrape," Gram answered for me. "Shouldn't even leave a scar, the doctor said."

Seth's smile warmed my insides like welcomed heat on a cold day. "I'm just glad she's okay."

He released me and went to my mother. "Susan, I promise you that Troy is going to be fine. He took a good crack to the head, but he's got a hard noggin. A few stitches fixed him up. He'll have a headache for a few days. Otherwise he's as good as new."

"Are you sure?" Mom asked, blowing into a tissue and snuffling, the fountain in her eyes finally shutting off.

"Positive."

"Thank God," Mom said, grabbing another tissue to dab at her damp cheeks. Her phone rang. She frowned as she pulled it from her purse, a look of dread crossing her face. "I have to take this. It's Hannah's parents. They're vacationing in Mexico. I've been trying to reach them all night."

I spotted Whitey standing in the doorway, looking like a man who didn't want to intrude, while wanting Mom to know that he was there if she needed him. He genuinely seemed to care about her. I decided that I might not know him all that well yet, and I hadn't really given him as much benefit of the doubt as I should, but I liked that he respected my mother's feelings. It went a long way in his favor.

Gram picked up the cold cups of coffee. "Whitey, why don't you and I fetch some fresh java while Susan finishes with that call?"

"Sure, Billie." He held his arm out to her, an old-fashioned gesture that Gram ate up.

"Come with me." Seth led me into the hall and out of CCU, his arm around my shoulders.

"Where are we going, Quinlan?" Not that I cared. At that moment, I'd go anywhere he wanted.

"You'll see."

An elevator ride later, we were in Troy's room. Meg and Sheriff Gooden were there. My best friend winked at me, as if what we'd all been through at the hands of a crazy woman was a walk in the park. But I noticed she stood at the head of Troy's bed, a hand on his upper arm. Something about her was different. It took me a moment to figure it out. Was that empowerment I saw twinkling in her big green eyes? Oh my God, it was. I felt a smile go all through me. My Meg was back.

But why did that make me want to cry? I mean, what did I expect? She'd been a hero, literally saving the day and my life. Probably all of our lives. I supposed that would definitely give somebody a large dose of self-confidence. I couldn't think of anyone who'd been needing that more than Meg. I returned the wink.

Nothing beats a best friend—except maybe a good man.

"You deserve to hear this, too, Daryl Anne," Troy said, his usually deep voice an octave higher. Probably pain meds. He gestured to the sheriff. "Okay, go on."

"Her real name," Sheriff Gooden said, checking a notepad, "is Cassandra Renee Wallace, but she goes by Cassie. According to the proprietor of the Veiled Bride in Portland, she worked at the store during the same time as Jenny Carson did. At first, Cassie seemed normal, but then she started to obsess about Jenny. She began dressing like her, got the same hairstyle, the same phone cover. The same everything.

"Apparently, Cassie was dumped by this Brad guy but was stalking him. Cassie blamed Jenny for the breakup, even though Jenny and Brad didn't meet until several months later. The day of Jenny and Brad's wedding, Cassie was caught trying to kill Jenny. Cassie ended up in Western State Hospital."

"How did she get from there to Weddingville?" Meg asked.

"She was recently accidentally released via clerical error," the sheriff said.

"She seemed so normal," Meg said.

Sheriff Gooden scratched his head as if it didn't make any sense whatsoever to him. But then, I supposed, he'd heard a lot of crazy things in his time in law enforcement. This was just one more. He said, "The department shrink says she could function normally because she was playing a role, the role of Jenny Carson, whose naval officer fiancé is deployed overseas, whose family lives in Gig Harbor, whose mother-in-law wants her to wear the hand-me-down wedding gown."

"Is the real Jenny Carson okay?" I asked, the horrific scene in the bridal shop still too vivid.

Troy said, "Yeah. She and Brad were married last year. He's stateside, stationed on the East Coast now."

Out of harm's way. Unlike Hannah. I prayed the surgery was going well.

"I don't get why she stole all those things," Meg said.

I knew the answer to that, thanks to my cousin. "She couldn't afford to pay for a wedding. She was 'borrowing' things to have the wedding she wanted."

Meg shook her head, pity in her eyes. "Why did she kill Willa Bridezilla?"

Sheriff Gooden cleared his throat. "Her doctor wouldn't give me any specifics about her delusions. Confidentiality and all. But the department shrink has a theory. He thinks when Cassie learned that Dillon dumped Lisa Marie for Willa, it triggered a new bout of psycho-something. Madness. It was so close to what had happened to her that in her mixed-up mind, she was being given a second chance to change the outcome. Willa needed to die. Dillon needed to realize he still loved Lisa Marie."

"Then why did she frame Lisa Marie?" I leaned back against Seth, my knees still a little shaky.

"This is where the new fantasy ran afoul of the original one. In real life, Cassie had been caught and locked away. In the new fantasy, Lisa Marie had taken on the role of Cassie. So Lisa Marie had to be caught and punished."

"And that meant there was no more Cassie, only Jenny, who was going to marry Brad," Troy said.

And she still thinks she's Jenny, I thought, shuddering. "How did Hannah become involved?"

Troy leaned back against the pillow, looking about done in.

He nuzzled Meg's hand. "Hannah found a lot of the stolen items from around town hidden in a box in the warehouse. She was going to show me last night. She got to the bridal shop before I did and caught Jenny setting up the salon for her 'perfect' wedding. If you'd arrived any later, she might not have made it. How's she doing?"

I checked my phone for a text, but so far nothing. I didn't know if that was good news or bad. "Still in surgery, I think."

The room was silent a moment; then Troy said, "When I arrived, Cassie caught me off guard, knocked me out. I didn't wake up until I was in the ambulance."

"Be glad." I wished I could erase the memory.

"Are you kidding!" Meg said. "You missed the best part. Me taking down that crazy bride with my new stun gun contraption. I was awesome."

"My hero," I said, meaning it.

"My love," Troy said, grinning at Meg. "Damn, I'd liked to have seen that."

"Hey," Seth said, "I think you can. That new security system Whitey put in will have recorded the whole thing."

"We'll need to see that," Sheriff Gooden said. "Evidence for the trial."

"Sheriff," Meg said, "about a certain ring that's stuck in the evidence room…"

Chapter 21

I've been to weddings that took years to plan, weddings that took nine months to plan, and weddings that took only weeks. But this is the first time I've attended or been part of a wedding that took mere days to put together.

"Perfection is overrated," Meg said. "Getting married is not about the wedding."

"It's not?" Could've fooled me. But then, since all things bridal were my forte these days, I was prejudiced.

"Nope." She shook her head, her fiery curls bouncing across her shoulders.

I'd thought Meg was beautiful the day she'd been going to marry Peter, but I was wrong. Today, she was like no one I'd ever seen before. And I'd seen some stunning actresses in L.A. But she was more gorgeous than words could express. The beauty wasn't only in the makeup, or the artfully done hair, or even the crimson slippers. There was a glow about her that was coming from inside, straight from a joyful heart.

I checked my own reflection in the mirror, liking the summery-blue maid-of-honor dress I wore. It seemed to brighten my eyes. I asked, "So, are you going to tell me what a wedding is about or not?"

"The marriage." She smiled a secret smile. "It's about life after the honeymoon. You don't need the most expensive gown, the biggest diamond, or to spend more than a house costs for a celebration."

"That's good to know, since I won't likely ever have that kind of money."

"You just need to find the right partner."

"And that's what you've done?" My doubts about Troy and Meg hadn't totally vanished. A tiny niggling doubt remained. I supposed because she hadn't out-and-out admitted that she totally trusted him yet.

"I've been so uncertain these last couple of months that I'm sure I've driven you as nuts as I've driven myself. But when I saw Troy unconscious and bleeding, I realized I couldn't live without him."

"You trust him, then?" I asked the hard question because that's what best friends do.

"Better. I trust me again." She laughed.

I joined in. "I'd hug you, but I don't want to ruin our makeup." We shared a hand squeeze. "No tears either."

"It's okay. I used smudge-proof mascara."

I felt a happy tear slip down my cheek. "Smudge-proof blusher, too?"

We laughed again.

A rap on the door. Meg's dad said, "It's time."

The whole town turned out, everyone except Hannah, who was still recovering and unable to leave her bed. There was standing room only in the church. Flora had come up with an array of blossoms that gave the chapel the look and feel of a summer garden in high bloom. Troy's dad was his best man, father and son as dashingly handsome as Hollywood leading men in black tuxedoes with sky-blue ties and cummerbunds.

Seth was taking photos, wearing his usual white dress shirt and suit pants with cameras for accessories. To me, he took top prize for best-looking male. Those chocolate eyes, that crooked grin, that giving heart. I won't lie. I might be prejudiced. I'd seen him naked, after all.

He stood near the entrance, capturing with his lens the moment the maid of honor started down the aisle, giving me a nod of approval that had my toes curling. As I stepped to the wedding march, he turned his attention to the bride and her father.

My best friend was getting married. It had never seemed so true or right as it did now, and my heart filled with delight.

Everyone in the chapel rose.

When the vows were said and Reverend Bell pronounced Troy and Meg husband and wife, the audience erupted with cheers. If ever a union was blessed, it was this one. The citizens of Weddingville had anticipated this event from the time these two were teenagers. The joyous wishes kept coming all through the reception.

The Gossip Sisters informed Seth that they wanted copies of the photos he was taking, even if they had to pay for them.

Lisa Marie showed up with a date, a Seattle businessman who bore no resemblance to the king of rock and roll. Just as well, since Dillon was doing an Elvis song or two from his routine later in the evening.

As toasts were given, I glanced at Meg's hand curled around the champagne glass. I imagined Granny O was smiling down on her great-grandson and his bride this day, knowing theirs would be a long and happy union, now that the ruby ring was where it belonged. On Meg's finger.

"A nickel for your thoughts, Blessing."

I slipped into Seth's arms with an ease that I no longer even questioned. "I was just thinking about something my best friend said to me earlier." *The important thing is the marriage. You just need the right partner.*

He held me close, swaying to the music, his gaze locked on mine. "Something you can share?"

"Maybe someday."

"Really? Someday? I bet I could get it out of you tonight."

I chuckled. "There's only one way you can finagle this out of me, Quinlan."

He bent close, his lips grazing my temple, his grin so sexy my insides began to melt. He whispered something naughty in my ear. "Is that the way?"

I blushed. "You're on the right path…"

He whispered something even more blush-worthy. "How about that?"

"Maybe…" Oh, who was I fooling? I couldn't pull off mysterious. Not with this face. I gave in, planting a kiss on his delicious lips. "How soon is too soon for the maid of honor to leave the reception?"

THE END

Did you miss Daryl Anne Blessing's first story?

See the next page for an excerpt from

A Wedding to Die For.

Chapter 1

The body came in on the noon tide just as the beach wedding reached a critical moment.

* * *

Three Days Before the Wedding

"Daryl Anne Blessing, you are the most wonderful maid of honor a bride could ask for," sobbed my best friend Meg Reilly.

Tears poured from her eyes like spring runoff from Mount Rainier as Meg collapsed in my arms. I staggered back, almost falling down the steps of the motel cottage, shock rippling through me. *The paramount duty of a maid of honor is to keep the bride emotionally calm.* Until this moment, I thought I was doing that.

Until this moment, I would have agreed with her praise of my maid of honor prowess. My short, black hair and blue eyes—the colors of a dark, calm sea—define my penchant for planning, organizing, and keeping everything on an even keel, and are the perfect foil to Meg's long fiery hair, flashing green eyes, and propensity for spur-of-the-moment chaos.

The sunny May day promised a warm afternoon, but at 7:00 a.m. in this small seaside town on Puget Sound, the temperature hovered around thirty-nine degrees. Meg was barefoot, her robe knee-length. I eased her out of the cold, damp morning air and back into the room that looked like a cheap Vegas wedding suite.

Possible causes for Meg's meltdown ran through my mind as I shut the door. Wedding gown, shoes, veil—ordered, arrived, fitting later today. Check. Bridesmaid's dresses, shoes, jewelry— all distributed. Check. My outfit. Check. Bridal shower—last weekend. Check. Bachelorette party. Tonight. Hmmm. Had the stripper canceled?

No. Wait. Meg said I was *wonderful*. That meant something else. Something…*good*? Then why the waterworks? "What's happened?"

Meg released me, sniffling. "*She's* coming."

If Meg had stabbed me, I would have been less stunned. My heart sank. Of all things good I could imagine happening to, or for, my best friend, *her* coming to the wedding was not one of them. God knows, I had nothing to do with it. I'd tried every argument I could think of to talk Meg out of inviting *her*.

I foresaw nothing but disaster in this news. I couldn't allow that. I had to minimize potential damage, but first I'd need more details, and as long as Meg was sobbing, I wouldn't get any.

My gaze raced around the compact room, my vision bombarded by every possible honeymooning couple's fantasy. Hearts and flowers and linked golden bands. Everywhere. I spied a box of tissues on the nightstand and handed one to Meg. I plastered on a smile. *The maid of honor's number one job is to keep the bride emotionally calm.* That meant keeping my opinion to myself. "Why are you crying? This is happy news, right?"

Meg daubed at her watery, green eyes, shoved her mop of long, red curls from her splotched face, and offered me a wobbly smile. "I know you're afraid she'll hurt me again, but it felt wrong not to invite her. After all, she's my mother."

Who ran out on you and your dad when you were eleven! I was there. I'd witnessed the broken child struggling to understand why her mother didn't want her. I hated that Meg struggled still with that sense of being unwanted that had shaped so many of her life choices.

I lost my dad the same year her mother left, and now a memory swept back. I'd escaped his funeral and its aftermath by stealing away to my favorite spot at the end of the dock. Seagulls cried overhead as though they shared my grief. Meg found me, sat down, and offered me candy and condolences. I'd thanked her, shared a long moment of silence, and then I'd turned to her and said, "You understand, don't you?"

We were at that awkward age, little girls not quite preteens, naïve about so many things. And yet there lurked something in Meg's eyes that was too wise for her years. "You mean 'cause we've both lost a parent? Yeah, it makes us the same."

I'd taken her hand, glad of her friendship, but intent on correcting her perception. "Not exactly the same. Your mom can always come home."

"No," she'd said, dead certainty in the word. "She won't. But if your dad could come back he would. He *loved* you."

She'd been right about her mother. Tanya had never come home. Never phoned. Never written. But now the bitch was coming to her wedding? My heart wrenched. Even though I wanted to shout down the rafters, my best friend needed me to set aside my animosity and put a positive spin on this. I firmed up my smile, but not one supportive word choked from my constricted throat.

"Every girl wants her mother at her wedding," Meg said, snuffling. "You'd want Susan at yours."

Yes, but I wasn't getting married. I wasn't even dating. And my mom wasn't a lying, cheating, family-deserting bitch on wheels. A widow for fifteen years, my mom still lived with her mother-in-law. My parental units put a premium on loyalty. As did I.

As did Meg.

I sighed inwardly. She needed my support now, not bawled out. I summoned courage. Fortitude. A best friend's twin superpowers at times like these. "As long as you're happy, Meg, I'm happy for you."

"Really?" Her smile was crooked and instantly endearing.

"Pinkie swear." We hooked little fingers as we'd been doing since grade school, then crossed our hearts to seal the deal.

"Now wash those eyes and get dressed, and do your makeup magic on that red nose. My body is craving caffeine and a stack of blueberry pancakes."

She stopped the trek across the cabin toward the bathroom, a look of dread crinkling her face. "Not Cold Feet?"

Cold Feet Café is the best place in town to sit down with a cup of your favorite brew and contemplate whatever needs contemplating. It's also Meg's father's business. I had another sinking feeling. "You didn't tell your dad before you sent the invitation, did you?"

She bit her lower lip, hugging her bathrobe. "I know you said I should, but I thought he'd object."

No shit, Sherlock. I suspected, though, she was mostly worried about hurting his feelings. That also worried me. Finn Reilly was the kind of big, strong guy who gave off the impression he could take on the world without blinking—unless you really looked at him and saw beyond the bluster. His quick smile never quite vanquished a dull pain in his eyes.

I had the niggling feeling something bad was brewing, and it wasn't coffee. "Okay, then, Jitters and a blueberry muffin."

While Meg dressed and fixed her hair and makeup, I sat on the bed lost in thought. It seemed such a short time ago that we'd graduated high school and took off to seek our fortunes in Hollywood. A couple of years in, she'd landed a job on a network sitcom as an assistant makeup artist and suggested they hire me as Key Wardrobe, the person in charge of what the actors wear each episode. Where had the time gone? In three days Meg would be married and—

"What are you ruminating about?" Meg said—all signs of a crying jag abolished by her incredible cosmetic finesse—pulling me back to the moment.

Just thinking how our lives are going to change forever once you say "I do," my friend, but I couldn't say that out loud. "Just thinking how much I really need some caffeine."

She laughed as we stepped outside into the bright sunshine. We both wore jeans and sweatshirts. If this were a TV episode, I would have selected these outfits for "two young women eating at a small-town diner." But there was more to it than dressing appropriately. Meg and I were minor celebrities in the hometown-girls-make-good spirit, one of us even marrying a big-name actor, and it was important not to appear to be putting on airs.

We linked hands as though holding tight to our friendship and started down the street. Meg said, "I'm so glad we're here together."

"To quote Dorothy," I said, "there's no place like home."

That made us both laugh. Our hundred-year-old seaside town, located near Fox Island in Pierce County, had come into existence when logging and fishing were mainstays of Pacific Northwest industry. As their economy flourished, the city founders—strapping young bachelors—commissioned a slew of mail-order brides. So many marriages took place the first year this Washington State town was established, it became known as Weddingville.

And the name stuck.

More recently, the town began to flounder. Income was down across the board. With one exception. Blessing's Bridal, the wedding-wear shop my mom and grandmother run. The city council met and discussed the dire situation and came up with a brilliant idea. Turn Front Street into something akin to an outlet mall—for weddings. A kind of one-stop-wedding-shopping experience, everything a bride, groom, or wedding planner could want in a single setting.

Local shopkeepers embraced the proposal, changing not only their merchandise accordingly, but also their storefronts. Jitters espresso stand became Pre-Wedding Jitters, Trudy's Lingerie became Her Trousseau, Ring's Jewelry became The Ring Bearer, Flora's Flowers became The Flower Girl, and so on. Motels were given honeymoon suite makeovers, some more tacky than others. The old community church and several outdoor locales became wedding ceremony sites.

Yes, there truly is "no place like home."

"Hey, this isn't the way to Jitters. Unless... did it move?"

"It didn't move. But you were right. I need to tell Dad."

My appetite fled. "Are you sure?"

"No, but I'm doing it anyway."

"Alrighty then." We trekked the four blocks downhill to Front Street. "After breakfast let's swing by Trudy's and pick out a couple of lacy bits guaranteed to make yours one hot, sexy honeymoon."

"Let's see how my talk with Dad goes first," Meg said, seeing right through my feeble attempt to keep her calm.

How did one tell the dad she adored that she'd invited the woman who'd run out on them fifteen years ago to her wedding? That the invitation was accepted? I shuddered inwardly. Big Finn Reilly was not going to take this well.

Cold Feet Café came into view. Perched on the waterside of Front Street, it shared the brick facade of many other buildings on this street. Cars angled into the curb, and the large windows revealed occupied booths and tables. "Oh God, Meg, the place is packed."

"It's just the usual breakfast crowd," she said, not sounding worried but biting her bottom lip, a sure tell.

I tried not to imagine the emotional tornado that was about to level this small-town diner. And failed. "Maybe you should put this off until the café is—"

"No way. If I put this off any longer, I'll explode."

If she didn't put this off, Big Finn might explode.

Meg swept inside with me on her heels. A bell over the door announced our arrival, but didn't dent the medium-level chatter, the clatter of silverware on plates, or the confluence of delicious aromas. Several folks offered welcome home greetings and congratulations to Meg, which we responded to in kind.

The decor was a cheery red and white with splashes of chrome. My nervous gaze found Big Finn. He stood behind the counter at the far end, deep in conversation with one of the diners. His crisp apron showed breakfast stains. Taller than most by six inches, he stood out like a red-topped evergreen in a forest of baseball-capped saplings.

I caught Meg's arm. "Maybe you should consider saving your news until he isn't so busy."

She wasn't swayed. "It's rip off the bandage time."

I gulped. A band tightened around my chest. I should go with her, but this was between Meg and her father. It was hard to stay where I was as Meg headed toward Big Finn. I felt like I was witnessing a train wreck in the making, yet unable to prevent it.

Halfway to her dad, Meg was stopped in her tracks by a woman with crayon yellow hair seated in one of the booths. "Oh, Meg, I was hoping to catch you here."

Zelda Love, our local wedding planner, patted a folder on the table that looked more like an overstuffed sandwich with its ingredients about to escape from all sides.

I felt a tug on my sleeve. "Oh, Daryl Anne?"

I glanced down at three women seated in a booth. They were my grandmother's age, her Bunko buddies. Velda Weeks had the flyaway gray hair of a fluffy dog and a grin like the Cheshire Cat about to lure Alice into trouble. "Sit, sit."

She indicated the empty spot beside her. I complied, giving them all a warm smile. "How are you?"

"We're more than a little curious," Jeanette Corn, a throwback to the hippie generation, admitted, her thin face more animated than usual. I swear she'd never cut her long hair or worn a touch of makeup. "We hear Meg is getting married."

I was pretty sure the whole town knew that by now.

"And she didn't invite any of us," Velda said, scowling her disapproval.

"I'm doing the cake," Wanda Perroni, the owner of The Wedding Cakery, an Italian bakery, snipped as though that gave her a one-up on Velda and Jeanette. "The smallest one in many years, I can tell you."

"What we want to know is who is this guy she's marrying? Why is it so hush-hush?" Velda asked.

"He must be someone important is what I say," Wanda said. "From Hollywood. A director or movie star. I'm right, aren't I?"

"I'll bet it's George Clooney," Velda said.

"He's married, Velda," Wanda said. "It's probably that guy who does those *Mission Impossible* movies. I hear he's single and looking."

"Meg can't marry him. She's Catholic," Jeanette said. She sighed and did a pretend swoon. "I hope it's that new James Bond. He's a dreamboat."

"I bet it's someone from TV," Velda said. "Like that sexy Shemar Moore on *Criminal Minds* who's always flirting with that computer whiz Garcia and calling her Baby Girl. Does Meg's fiancé call her Baby Girl?"

I sat in stunned silence. I wasn't happy they knew Meg's fiancé was an actor. We'd tried hard to keep that under wraps, but I admired their attempts to get me to spill the beans. TMZ had nothing on the gossips in this town. "Ladies, I can't tell you anything. I've been sworn to secrecy."

"I always thought Meg would marry Troy," Jeanette said. Her friends agreed.

I needed to make an escape without more questions and without offending my gram's friends. But how?

"Does Troy know Meg's getting married?" Velda asked.

Behind me, the doorbell tinkled, and a familiar voice called, "Daryl Anne?"

I said a silent "Thank you, God" and exited the booth, reaching the door to greet my paternal grandmother. Wilhelmina

Blessing—known to one and all as Billie—was tall and reed thin, her black hair twisted into its usual chignon, her blue eyes bright with excitement. She wore her favorite Chanel pantsuit, the right sleeve pushed up to accommodate the removable cast on her wrist.

She gave a few friendly waves, greeted her Bunko buddies, then steered me toward the counter. "Come on, I could use a cuppa."

"Me too," I said, glad for the company, even if adding caffeine to my already anxious nerves might not be such a great idea. I settled onto a stool beside her. "How's the wrist this morning?"

"A little weak." Billie did all the alterations for Blessing's Bridal, and she'd taught me how to sew when I was old enough to hold a needle and thread it. Six weeks ago, she'd slipped and broken her wrist, bringing me home from Los Angeles earlier than planned to help out in the bridal shop. Although the doctor pronounced her all healed last week, she claimed she wasn't taking chances. Thus the removable cast.

I suspected, however, it was a ploy to keep me home longer. Sadly, I was returning to L.A. the day after the wedding. I kissed her cheek, knowing how much I would miss doing that once I was back in California.

We ordered coffee, the old-fashioned kind, then she said, "You forgot to turn on your phone. I kept getting voice mail."

"I'm sorry." I'd turned off my phone when Meg was having her meltdown. I pulled it from my pocket, turned it on, noting a couple of missed calls from Gram, but nothing else that required my immediate attention. I stirred cream into my coffee. "What's up? Is everything okay?"

"Fine. Better than fine." She stirred artificial sweetener into her coffee. "Exciting even. You know that reporter who's coming to interview everyone in town for that series of articles?"

"Yes." This advertising opportunity was more than a few

articles. It was an Internet broadcast associated with a national network. I'd viewed a couple of sample shows, and it looked like a good deal that might benefit Blessing's Bridal as well as several other businesses in town.

"Well, we just got an e-mail from TR Jones," Billie said, setting her spoon on the saucer and ordering us each a warm, gooey cinnamon roll without asking if I wanted something else. I guessed the blueberry pancakes could wait for another day, but I raised an eyebrow at her selection.

She had Type 2 diabetes and Mom watched like a hawk over every bite of sugar that went into her mouth. Billie hated being told she couldn't do something and, even though it often led to disaster, like a broken wrist, she ignored what others thought was good for her and did whatever she damn-well pleased. Usually I admired that about her.

But not when it came to her health. She ignored my raised brow, forked a bite of cinnamon roll, and sighed with pleasure. "He wants to do our interview today. Now, before you protest, I didn't forget about Meg's final fitting or your girls' plans. So I figured early was better than later, get it over and done with, then you'll have the rest of the day free."

She sounded as though she was doing me a favor, and her look said, "I've already set this up so please say *yes*." She lifted her cup and peered over its rim. "Okay?"

I thought about saying: *Sure. Why not? Why should anything go according to my plans today?* But I was not a martyr, and there was Meg to consider. She and Zelda still had their heads together discussing some last-minute details of the wedding or reception. And then she would talk to Big Finn. The cinnamon roll began to congeal in my stomach. Maid of honor duties aside, I couldn't just desert my best friend in her hour of need.

"What time did you tell him?"

She glanced at the clock over the door. "Nine o'clock."

It was 8:30. Barely enough time for us to get back to Blessings Bridal and for me to change clothes to something more suitable for an interview.

Billie gobbled down the last of her cinnamon roll as I pushed mine aside half eaten.

I said, "I'll have to tell Meg."

Billie's cell phone rang. "Your mother," she said. She answered, and the color drained from her face. "What? Are you sure?"

She handed me the phone. "She wants to speak to you."

"Mom, is something wrong?"

"Depends on your definition of right."

"What does that mean?"

"The people from the Internet are here with their cameras and lights and—"

"Oh, no. Tell them I'll be right there."

"It's not *them* you need to concern yourself with. It's *her.*"

"*Her?*"

"The woman writing the articles."

I swear I heard venom in Mom's voice.

I frowned. "I thought the reporter was a man, a TR Jones."

"That's what she's calling herself these days, but she's still Tanya Reilly."

My mouth dropped open, and just as a hush fell over the café, I blurted out, "Meg's mother?"

From the end of the counter, I saw Big Finn's head snap in my direction.

Thank You

Gail Fortune—I could not have imagined, when we first met, that years later you would be the person I can always count on to have my back. Fate drew us together, but respect and caring have woven a strong bond between us. Thank you for being my friend and for being the best agent I could ever want.

Alex Logan—I love that we share a love of cats and romantic mysteries. I am grateful every day for your red pencil, for your sense of humor, and for your hard work above and beyond on my behalf. I know I'm repeating myself, but the universe really did smile on me the day you became my editor. Thank you for always making this journey easier.

Karen Papandrew—your belief in me is more appreciated than I can put into words. Your loyalty and encouragement have seen me through some pretty tough times, and I thank you so much for caring about me no matter what. You define the word *friend*.

Larry and the two cats, Fuzzy and Spooky—for providing cheap entertainment.

FOREVER

Looking for More Books
by Adrianne Lee?

Don't Miss the Big Sky Pie Series